"Because I care. I just do. I—Rebekah, I *need* you for my wife."

"Cook, washerwoman, such as that?"

"More than that. Listen. There's something I haven't told you. Maybe it won't mean much to you now, but I have to tell you. You see, my whole name is Isaac Aden Robards. Remember Isaac and Rebekah in the Bible?"

"Yes. Abraham sent for a wife for his son, Isaac, and the servant brought back Rebekah. I never understood how Rebekah could leave her home and go with a stranger that way. It didn't make a bit of sense."

"No. I guess it didn't," he said. "Because you haven't learned yet about following God's leadings."

"And what is that supposed to mean? That I'm not spiritual enough?"

"We all have room to grow, don't we?" he asked.

"Well. Sure. But what do our names have to do with this? Surely you don't think—I mean this is 1881 in Georgia, not 'whatever' B.C. in the Promised Land. And anyway, you're Isaac yourself. If you wanted to do a reenactment, you should have sent your servant. Or is there a hidden master somewhere? Are you really the servant?"

"Please don't laugh. Although I guess it does sound pretty funny. But I'm absolutely serious about this. And I'm not trying to stage a reenactment. I know the analogy isn't complete. This is what's happened. God has shown me He'd give me a wife and I'd know who it is because, aside from His telling me in my heart, her name would be Rebekah."

Rebekah put her hand to her mouth. "You can't make decisions based on—"

"A word from the Lord? Absolutely. It's the safest way of doing business, simply obeying the Lord."

"Oh. So this is business, is it?"

BRENDA KNIGHT GRAHAM and her veterinarian husband live in Georgia, the setting for most of her stories. Mother of two and grandmother of two, she has been crafting tales since she was seven years old.

Books by Brenda Knight Graham

HEARTSONG PRESENTS
HP158—On Wings of Song

Her Name Was Rebekah

Brenda Knight Graham

Heartsong Presents

Dedicated to
J.B. and Elizabeth with love.

Special thanks to Thomas K. Leggett, Jr., DMD, for obtain-
ing a copy of *Dentistry:An Illustrated History* by Malvin E.
Ring, DDS; my aunt Emma Berrong, aged 104, for notes on
Cornelia and apples; and for overwhelming support—
Annette, Audrey, Charles, Deidre, Jackie, Julie, and Sue.

A note from the author:
*All characters in this story are fictitious. However, my family
history does boast an Isaac in upstate New York who came
south looking for his Rebekah—and found her! I love to hear
from my readers! You may correspond with me by writing:*

Brenda Knight Graham
Author Relations
PO Box 719
Uhrichsville, OH 44683

ISBN 1-58660-613-1

HER NAME WAS REBEKAH

All Scripture quotations are taken from the King James Version of
the Bible.

All of the characters and events in this book are fictitious. Any
resemblance to actual persons, living or dead, or to actual events
is purely coincidental.

Cover illustration by Victoria Lisi and Julius.

one

Rebekah Thornton sifted flour into mountain peaks in a dark, troughlike wooden bowl. Thumping the sifter against the bowl's edge, she watched as tall mountains collapsed into nothing but a wilderness of bran-speckled bread flour. She idly made a squiggle line through that expanse with one finger. Mother once would have disapproved of Rebekah's baking on Sunday afternoon. But even if Mother would care now, she was taking a nap. The whole log dogtrot house was so quiet, now that the squeaky sifter was still, that she could hear nothing but a gossipy chatter of chickens grubbing the backyard and a teakettle's soft hiss of steam. She dug out a handful of lard from a barrel, added it with warm yeasty water to her wilderness of flour, and, with milk for mixing, soon had developed what she called "some really nice, good dough."

Aside from roaming outdoors, baking bread was the very best activity she could choose in preparation for talking to Father. She'd have hot bread to offer him later if he were upset, and kneading dough would soothe her own nerves. Talk to him she must. Working fields with him every day surely gave her the right to know what was happening to their beloved farm, Thornapple.

When she'd set dough to rise in pans, she threw her apron over a chair back as she left the kitchen to cross a hallway, called a "dogtrot" because it extended clear through the house, open at each end to the outdoors. An open, rough-hewn staircase ascended from one side with a clapboard door at the top to protect occupants from the elements. She dashed up those steps now, taking them two at a time as she hiked her dress up a notch. It would be best to shine up a bit before facing Father.

He never liked her to be less than a lady on Sunday, no matter how grubby she might become on Monday.

Carefully considering her three decent dresses, Rebekah chose the dimity with blue flowers. It was too early to wear such a summery thing, Mother would say, but it was one Father really liked, and right now that was what was important. Anyway, the day was warm, and, though lightweight, the dress had long sleeves and a high neck.

Rebekah, being a tall girl, had to stoop slightly in her attic room to see her reflection in a mirror so mottled she had to twist this way and that to see herself between bluish mars in the glass. She'd always called those shapes land masses and bodies of water like segments of a map. Virginia stood alone on one side; then there was a long stretch of Atlantic Ocean lapping against Georgia's coastline right down the middle, and below that a perfect cratered moon. Her reflection confirmed that, yes, her dark hair tumbling in an unruly mass should be put up. She rubbed a smudge of flour off her cheek and grabbed her brush.

Settling into a small armless rocker, she began to plait her hair into a single long braid. Mother would have had her braid it before she made the bread, but she hadn't thought about it then. Maybe there wouldn't be a hair in the dough! The mindless movement of her fingers weaving in and out of silky strands gave her ample time to consider her talk with Father. She'd waited all day, given him hours to recover from his three-day trip to Athens. She'd watched him last night take his horse to the barn and return with feet dragging and had decided he was far too tired for her to trouble then, no matter how she longed to.

But now she had to know why Robinsons' Feed and Seed had refused to let her buy spring planting supplies on credit as they'd always done before. It was 1881, a very promising year. She and Father had read together many times Henry W. Grady's glowing words in Atlanta's *Constitution* about a wonderful future for the South. Sure, farmers were being urged to diversify, to plant less cotton and more corn. And they had done that. Last year they'd planted only two acres in cotton, the rest in corn. And Father had been pleased with the results. Mr. Robinson's excuse that it wasn't a good year for credit simply didn't hold water. Somehow she knew he meant not that it was a bad year for everyone but for Thornapple in particular.

Thornapple. What a funny name for the Thornton family farm near Hogansville, Georgia. The story was that when Father and Mother came from North Carolina to settle here in 1857, Mother had insisted on naming it Thornapple, though Father argued that thornapples were little trash trees, and her choice wouldn't be a very flourishing name to start out with. Mother was a romantic and had liked the sound of it and the way it used a large portion of their name, Thornton. Now Mother didn't remember her own name many days, much less the name of their farm. Worse than forgetting mere names was Mother's forgetfulness of who they were, that Father liked poached eggs on toast, that Josh wasn't here but away at the university in Athens, and that she, Rebekah, would rather plow any day than be dressed up in petticoats and frills. Even when Mother was well, Rebekah had seldom asked her for advice. She'd always felt more protective of her mother than expecting help from her. And certainly now she couldn't go to her with her feelings of helpless dread that something awful was about to happen to Thornapple.

She descended the steps slowly, unconsciously avoiding creaky boards, sliding one hand lightly along a skinned pole stair rail. When she stood before Father's study door, she suddenly forgot all the bold questions she'd framed. She looked to her left along wide, pine floorboards to the opening at the dogtrot's end and out past branches of a large oak to a slack-wired weed-grown fencerow, and beyond that to dark red furrows of a freshly plowed field. She'd laid out the last straight row in that field yesterday and had itched to begin planting it and other prepared fields. But when she'd tried to get guano fertilizer on Father's credit, she was denied. Nor would they talk about letting her get a new planter or even the coffee Mother often requested. And why?

She made a hard fist and knocked on the door.

"Come!"

Father looked up briefly from his farm record books, tried a smile that didn't even tickle his steel gray mustache, and said, "Oh. Rebekah. Have a seat."

She clutched rough brown hands in her white dimity lap and leaned forward in her chair. "Did you have a good trip, Father?"

"Sure. Good as could be, I guess." He didn't look up.

"Was Josh all right?"

"Oh. Yes. Josh—is—fine."

"Father." She stood up in such a hurry, her chair fell over backward. "You can tell me the truth. I'm not a little girl any longer, you know. I'm twenty now."

He looked up then, blue eyes startled. "Really, Rebekah, has something gone wrong while I was away? You seem extremely jittery. I thought your mother seemed about the same as I left her."

"Oh, yes, Mother's fine—well, as fine as you can expect. I've taken good care of her. I got Nancy West to stay with her while I went to town yesterday. But *I'm* not fine, and I won't be until you tell me what's going on!" She picked up her fallen chair and sat back down with a thump, wishing with all her might she could remain calm.

"You went to town yesterday? I thought I told you—"

"But we'd decided to use that guano this year, remember? And we need a new planter. The one we have has that broken handle, and half the time it won't drop the seeds when it should and then drops a wad of them. You weren't home yet, so I thought I should go for things." She waved a hand westward, then eastward. "The fields are ready to plant! Mr. Jones planted his corn three weeks ago—"

"Rebekah!" It was her turn to be startled. Father seldom raised his voice like that.

He heaved to his feet and pulled at his mustache as he maneuvered his way around his desk. When he stopped and leaned one hip against his desk, he looked down at her, and Rebekah noticed for the first time how his eyes appeared swollen, his skin saggy and gray. He put a hand to his deeply furrowed brow as if to rub away a nagging pain, then used the same hand to grip the desk edge.

She shouldn't have needled him so. But what could be wrong?

"Rebekah," said Father in a thick voice, "I—didn't want to tell you this, but—I have to. The bank is foreclosing on Thornapple. We're losing the farm."

"No! It's not possible! You own this farm! You've always said whatever happened we'd have the farm because it's paid for. You said that, Father!"

"Well, there are such things as mortgages, Child. To help you pay for other things you can't—afford."

"Like what? Our crops have been good! What couldn't we pay for? Father?"

He rubbed his eyes with both hands as if to clear a cloudy picture, then brushed his stubby fingers through a stand of short gray hair before propelling himself into pacing to the window and back, again and again.

"Father, tell me! What has happened?" When he still didn't answer, she suddenly knew. "It's Josh, isn't it? Something's happened to Josh."

"He's all right. But he won't be in school anymore. And—"

"And what? What does this have to do with Thornapple? We could use Josh to help us. Is he coming back?" Under ordinary circumstances, they would have had a laugh at the mention of Josh being any help on the farm. As of her last knowledge, he'd probably freeze before he could even figure out how to build a fire.

But there was no laughter. The pacing stopped beside her.

"Rebekah, promise me you'll still love your brother. People do things; they just do things sometimes. You know—he wanted to be a doctor, and he was smart enough. But he couldn't bear the sight of blood. He wanted to be a lawyer—and he'd have been good. But he couldn't stay awake long enough at night for all that reading. And then—"

"He was going to finish his business degree and—"

"And open a men's clothing store in Hogansville." Still no glimmer of humor in his gray voice. They both knew quite well that Hogansville needed a men's clothing store about as much as it needed a millinery shop or a fancy hotel. Everyone shopped at Drew's General Store and Robinsons' Feed and Seed. That was it.

"Father. Just tell me. What's Josh done? What's happened?" His pacing had brought him close to her chair. She tugged at his sleeve as she'd done since she first followed him beside the plowing mules. He patted her shoulder awkwardly as if all of a sudden she'd become that little tomboy again. Then he turned quickly back toward the window.

"It started out as innocent gambling for pennies. Just for fun. But—"

"Josh has been gambling?"

"Yes. For—a long while," he said. "Poker games and such."

A rooster crowed outside. She waited for the rest of the story while folding tiny pleats in a section of her soft skirt. Her mouth was dry. She'd go to the spring for water when this was over. When this was over?

"He gambled—everything away," Father continued. "The farm, the cattle, everything, I'm afraid. He's—devastated by it, refuses to come home. He's going to Atlanta to try to get work. Knows somebody down there he thinks can help. I told him—I had to, he should have known that—I told him I couldn't help him anymore. Rebekah, think how awful he has to feel!"

She jumped to her feet and put her hands on her hips. "I know how we would feel, but I'm not sure Josh feels anything at all except sorry that the game's over. I'm sorry, Father, if I can't be very compassionate right now. But we have to save Thornapple. You can do that, can't you? At least part of it. We can do a lot with just a few acres. You know, with that guano fertilizer we can make the most beautiful crops. Like Mr. Jones's. Even if we lose some of the farm, we can hang onto some of the best acreage. And this house. Of course we can!"

"I'm trying. But I see no way. And you know—your mother is far from well anyway. How can we keep her safe while both of us work fields? I'd already been wondering what we were going to do. And now—" He pulled a crumpled letter from his pocket. "This is from your mother's sister, your aunt Constance in LaGrange. She wants us to come live with her, has been asking us to move there for fifteen, sixteen years, ever since the war when she lost your uncle Herbert. Don't look so stricken, Rebekah! Don't make this any harder than it already is!"

"Don't look stricken, you say! Am I supposed to be delighted about all this? You've let my brother gamble away the farm I'd have given my life for! And I cannot go live in town with Aunt Constance!"

"You're quite right. Constance has only enough room for your mother and me. We'll arrange something else for you."

"Arrange something? Arrange something! You're telling me I'm losing my home, my parents, everything, all in one fell swoop?" She choked on her words. It was just too preposterous!

Father walked again to the tall, curtainless window, his slumped shoulders dark against the bright western sky. He'd always refused to have curtains because he wanted to see everything, from puppies rolling in the sun to clouds drifting over. And he was going to live in LaGrange? Would Aunt

Constance let him have a curtainless window? This plan was no better for him than for her. It simply wouldn't work.

"Father, I'm not leaving this place—not now—not ever."

"Rebekah, your whole life is before you, and you don't need to be so melodramatic about this," he said, turning once more and putting his hands out, palms up. "I know you have a number of young beaus around here who already have been trying to work up courage to propose marriage. Surely one of them is suitable for you. I can arrange for you to stay with the Joneses until—"

"Until the right one kneels at my feet? Until my heart goes pitty-pat and everything is perfect? I will never marry, Father! Thornapple is all I want! I'm staying right here! No one is going to move me!"

"You can't. The farm will no longer be ours. The estate sale is set a week from Friday."

"Estate sale? You—and you still weren't going to tell me? Oh, Father!"

"Get hold of yourself, Rebekah. Show some faith, can't you? I'll talk to Mr. Jones tomorrow. He's always seemed to manage without making his girls do heavy work. Maybe you can learn to play their piano, let your hands soften up a bit."

"Father, you don't even know me. I thought you understood me. I—I can't believe you've let this horrible thing happen! But, regardless—well, no one is going to make me leave, and I don't want soft hands!"

She gripped the doorknob and realized her hand was shaking as if she had a bad chill. She took one last look at Father, who, with infuriating calmness, was sitting back down behind his desk. A slant of late sunshine turned his short, gray hair a pinkish tinge and threw his prominent features into harsh relief as he stared down at columns of spidery entries. It was all she could do to keep from slamming the door, but she knew even in her distress she didn't want to upset Mother.

Her own words echoed in her mind as she raced her horse, Firefly, between fields ready for planting. "I won't leave! No one can make me leave!" Were those empty, meaningless words? What would happen to these fields? Would someone else plant this year? No one else would love it the way she did. No one else would care for the sweep and tilt of the fields or the fringes of woods whose tall straight pines gave you sights for aiming straight rows. Oh, they'd care how much per acre the land yielded, but they wouldn't appreciate the color of rich reddish earth, the bravery of tender green shoots standing at attention in long furrows.

Show a little faith, Father had said! Faith? What was that? All she knew was that if there was a God, of which she'd never been sure, He certainly cared not a flip about little helpless creatures He'd randomly set in motion. If she'd pictured God at all, she'd thought of Him as being like Cousin Isabel, who always wanted to play paper dolls when she came to visit. She'd set the dolls up in all sorts of little scenes, and then when she got tired, she'd simply sweep them down with one hand, laughing at her own game.

Anyway, who was Father to say have a little faith, when he had never shown much interest in that area of life? Oh, he went to church. But Rebekah knew he dreaded it every week and simply did it to make her mother happy—and for appearances, traditions. She'd never seen him studying his Bible.

The sun was setting behind her, and her own shadow careened ahead of her. Darkness thickened between trees far to her left beyond plowed ground. The scent of dark, vulnerable earth turned up to the sun had always made her feel so good, challenged in a contented kind of way. Now she shook her head as if to shed the scent, to rid herself of an untrue message. She urged Firefly to jump a gully and then slowed as she ascended a hill she'd dubbed Monarch Mountain because of butterflies she once found there. At the top of the hill was an open area where one could see out, view low, blue hills rippling away to beyond yonder. She stopped a moment and shaded her eyes to look west, where the simple shingled roof and stone chimney of Thornapple House glowed in the sunshine as if a painter had brushed them with gold. But where sunshine hadn't reached, under eastern eaves, in the kitchen's chimney corner, darkness was as dense as charcoal.

As she looked, everything gradually blurred. She bit her lip and firmed her chin, determined not to cry. Not yet. Flicking her braid over her shoulder, she pressed her knees against Firefly's warm sides and leaned toward the horse's head, turning east. She knew exactly where she was going. The same place she'd always gone with childhood woes, growing-up pains, and a young woman's heartaches. She was heading into woods and the very back acres of Thornapple, riding toward the Talking Tree.

two

Isaac Aden Robards heard a creaking, wrenching sound and looked back in time to see his covered wagon's left back wheel breaking away from its axle, idly lying down on the side of the road like a tired hound dog. The horses halted with a snort as their load suddenly became immovable.

"All right there, Jake, Jolly—what's up? Let me take a look," he reassured them as he leaped down. Hmm. That wheel was going to need a smithy before it would go again. How it had been rolling for the last ten miles was beyond him. He scratched his head and looked around. Not a soul in sight, not a house or a plume of smoke anywhere. It was nearing sunset on a Sunday afternoon, and everyone was at home tending their own business.

He whistled a hymn tune as he clumped about inspecting the area for a camping spot. Looked like a good place, a meadow opening out between trees and a stream murmuring nearby. A very good place. "Thank You, Lord, for this and many favors," he said, casting his gaze upward for a moment before heading back to the wagon.

Life as a traveling dentist in 1881 was not lucrative but full of adventure. It was amazing how people clung to their rotten teeth, not wanting to let even a slim dime pass between their fingers. Yet he spent little on himself, so he'd saved for the future nearly all he'd received. And, anyway, it was the life he felt called to in spite of his mother's objections. She'd never dreamed he would leave a healthy living as an apple grower in upstate New York to become a dentist with no home but his wagon. But she couldn't continue to argue with him once he convinced her that God was telling him to spread the gospel while tending people's toothaches. He'd have a captive audience, he explained to her with his crooked grin and lift of a shoulder. So she stood on tiptoes to hug him, pressed her face hard against his briary cheek, and then stood back and gave him a symbolic push on his chest. Sometimes, even now after two years in school, another practicing with a Pittsburgh dentist, and then this last year on the road, he found himself wiping a stray tear away as he thought of his widowed mother's loneliness managing the apple orchards by herself.

But he had to do this. That compelling force rolled him out every morning to seek new patrons and offer his services. Once he'd established himself, he usually had a goodly number of takers who helped him spread the news that a dentist was in town. He'd park under an oak tree on the town square or in front of a general store, anywhere he felt he'd have some traffic and not offend anyone. He had one good chair, not a dental chair, but that would come later. He would pull that chair out and set it by his wagon. Then he'd arrange a towel on a small metal table, bring out a black case full of instruments, and he was ready. On rainy days store owners sometimes allowed him a corner in their establishments. If not, he stretched out in his wagon with a good book and enjoyed his day off.

He talked about the Lord as he mined around in a client's mouth, or sometimes he'd cut loose singing "The Old Rugged Cross" or "Amazing Grace." Some folks left his wagon grinning even while cupping a hand over a painful jaw. Others invited him to their homes for a hot meal for which he was powerfully grateful. But some left in a grump as if all their pain were his fault. Every day was a brand-new adventure.

He smiled to himself now as he thought about his secret dream he hadn't even shared with Mother. She, even as devout a Christian as she was, wouldn't have understood his conviction that God would show him somewhere in his travels the girl he should marry. She'd have been sure he could find his bride right there in apple country. And he was shy about telling even her the clue by which he'd know "this is the one." Some divine messages were mighty hard to explain. This one was between him and God for now—until he found her.

He took up whistling the same tune where he'd left off a few minutes before, "In the sweet by and by, we shall meet on that beautiful shore. . . ." Considering priorities of the tasks before him, he set to work to get his wagon out of the road first. It took some shoulder shoving and some grunting, but he and the horses managed to get the crippled thing out of the way of any other possible traffic. His wagon was loaded with dental supplies, including a new case of mouthwash he'd bargained for back in Atlanta and his own personal belongings such as a bedroll and a box of books. The box of books he kept in the cradle of a small upside-down mahogany table he'd acquired in a toothy trade. He'd told one client who spied the table and wanted to buy it that he could have his bedroll, his food, and almost anything else in his wagon. The table, though, and the books, including his Bible, stayed. The table with its rich red grain, its curved legs, and its small drawer with a brass pull gave substance to his dream of having a home. Knowing it was there made him happy.

He unhitched his horses and made them comfortable. Still seeing no one, he decided it could do no harm to let Jake and Jolly graze a little. Whoever owned this land would surely not mind. He felt lighter himself when he gave each horse a slap on the rump and watched them take a little run through the trees, circle back, and begin some serious nibbling. He usually tethered them, but sometimes, like today, he couldn't resist giving them unfettered pleasure.

Now it was time to consider his own comforts. He gathered a goodly supply of crackly branches and started a fire with the help of his two fire-starting flint stones. A gnawing in his stomach demanded attention. He had those three potatoes a woman had given him for pulling her daughter's two front teeth. Only three potatoes, but they were nice ones. He could eat all three roasted under some coals. Or he could stew that old shriveled turnip, but he didn't relish that at all. The third alternative was to make porridge from some cornmeal. But that seemed better left for breakfast. Potatoes won.

He lay back to relax a bit while his potatoes cooked. He was studying cloud shapes and seeing how many different trees he could identify when he realized suddenly that the horses were completely out of sight and he couldn't hear their comfortable cropping any longer. He'd be in one ridiculous pickle if he lost his horses. They'd never left him before, but this might be the time when they yielded to an equine urge to run wild. He walked toward the thicket near which he'd last seen them.

He ambled through a stand of pines, needle carpet thick and soft under his feet, into another meadow similar to the one where he'd set up camp. Broom sedge rippled like golden wheat in a breeze. Woods surrounded the meadow on all sides. Almost in the center of the broom sedge meadow stood the most gorgeous red pine he'd ever seen. It was like a single dancer on stage poised and ready to perform. Or, he thought, it could be an enormous Christmas tree. But a lady in a sweeping bell of a skirt was the best description. There were few openings in dense, dark foliage to expose the trunk inside.

Spying his horses grazing not far away, nibbling with such contentment on tender grass growing under the broom sedge, he thought he'd leave them be for a bit. Looking around at the soft waist-high grass, then up at a blue sky full of pink, green, and gold sunset streamers, he knew what he wanted to do. He would lie on his back in the grass and watch sunset ships as he'd done when a child. He'd left a good bed of coals to roast those potatoes, and they'd be fine with no prodding for a little while.

The ground was cool and damp beneath him, but he felt hugged by the tall broom straw. And he loved the feeling of being able to watch the sky from such a private hiding place. Not that anyone was around anyway. Or was someone?

What was that sound? He knew the sounds to expect: distant running water; birds fluttering back and forth, hunting a last feed before dark; tiny tree frogs tuning up for an evening performance; the munch of his horses eating; a soft, whispery breath of a breeze in satiny, fur-tipped straw. But he heard another sound that didn't fit the scene at all, a sort of murmuring like the rise and fall of voices in conversation. Should he get up? But he was comfortable! Probably it was someone passing on the road. Or maybe his imagination. He'd just convinced himself of the latter and transported himself in imagery to riding a pink cloud when he realized he could even distinguish words. Yes. It was a woman, and she was inside the sweeping skirt of that pine tree. *What in the world—?* Why would she be out here in the middle of nowhere with darkness coming on?

Before he could spring up from his cave in the straw, he heard her—yes, it certainly was a woman—cry out as if she'd been stung or bitten. But what she said in a hard, emphatic tone was, "I'll never leave here! I just won't leave. You cannot make me go."

Now he was in a quandary. His instincts told him to dash to the aid of this person, whoever she was, and defend her against whomever was trying to remove her. But he heard no answering voice. As if she were alone. Now if he sprang to her rescue, it would scare her out of her wits and likely wouldn't make her too happy.

"Oh, Tree, how could he do this to us?" she cried again.

She was talking to the tree. Oh, my! She'd definitely not want to be overheard. Who was trying to make her go—from where? She needed help surely. But he couldn't just burst up out of the straw and offer his services. Instead he rose on his knees and, pointing himself dog-fashion toward his camp, started crawling. He was back in darkness of thicket when he heard her horse greeting his. So—she wasn't destitute. She had a horse.

Whistling then, he walked in forced nonchalance toward his horses, as if just discovering the place.

Sure enough, she came flouncing out of that pine tree like something wild, a force of bees stirred up or a bear routed from hibernation. Large brown eyes grew even larger when she saw him. She clamped a hand over her mouth and stared for a long moment, which should have given him time to think of something to say, but he could not. Like the time he'd fallen from a ladder and couldn't breathe, life stood still. She was a tall woman, twentyish probably, with high cheekbones and skin the color of his mother's prettiest loaves of light brown bread. Now she was calling her horse Firefly. Now she was mounting effortlessly even in that full dress of hers, not into a sidesaddle, but quite graceful all the same. In a flash she in her pale soft dress would be gone. And he could not make his tongue work.

She spoke quietly to her horse and started away, then turned back. Her thick, long braid swung around her chin as she turned, and she flipped it back over her shoulder. He still couldn't get his voice to work. He'd never seen anyone so beautiful. Or so unhappy. Those dark eyes were so devoid of sparkle.

"Don't you know you're trespassing?" she asked.

"Oh. I'm sorry. My wagon broke down." He waved his hand in the direction of his camp, then took one cautious step toward her. "Uh. My name's Aden Robards. I'm a dentist, a—traveling dentist."

She smiled suddenly, flashing even white teeth. "We don't need a dentist here."

"I see." He made an effort at keeping his hands hanging at his sides in what he hoped was a nonthreatening stance. "But of course. I'm the one who has needs. I've broken a wheel, need some blacksmith help. Any idea who I could get?"

"Probably Mr. Jones would help you. Mr. Millard Jones. He's down the road maybe a mile. He's—he'd be glad to help you. In the morning. You'd better be gone by tomorrow afternoon." She started away again as if that threat had settled everything.

"But wait!"

She half-turned with a calming word to her horse, but no word to Aden, only a lift of her dark eyebrows. Her horse pawed at the grass. One small pressure from his mistress's knee and he'd be gone.

Aden licked his dry lips. "Your name?" he asked. "I'd sure like to know to whom I'm indebted."

"That's totally unnecessary," she said, lifting her chin a bit higher.

"But—Mr. Jones. I need to tell him who sent me."

"Oh. Well, then. Rebekah Thornton sent you," she called as she galloped into the shadows and disappeared.

He stood watching her leave with his heart thundering as loudly, he felt, as her horses' hooves.

Her name was Rebekah.

three

Maybe it was a foolish thing to do when they were losing the farm, but she had to do something more progressive than everyday chores, more cheerful than packing dishes in crates. She simply had to get out and do something to produce growth, something connected to the earth. So she was setting out onions in the house garden plot. Then she'd plant squash and okra seeds she'd saved from last year's crop. Someone would have vegetables, even if she were gone. She had on her worst dress, an old grayish lavender thing that couldn't be any uglier even if pressed into the earth under her knees. It was a good feeling, the earth beneath her knees and vibrant between her fingers.

Finishing one row with a final pat over an onion, she stood to survey her work before moving her bucket of bulbs to the next row. She rubbed at the small of her back, knowing what her grimy hand would do to her dress but not caring in the least. It was at that moment she heard a foreign sound, maybe a squeak of leather or a sand-muffled hoofbeat. Then the dogs exploded into frantic barking in the front yard, and the chickens began squawking in the back.

Father had left for town straight from the breakfast table, and Mother would be frightened if no one were with her when visitors rode up. What if it were the banker? How did these horrible things, these foreclosures, take place anyway? Rebekah scurried in the back door. She dared not pause to wash in the basin beside the door.

She found Mother standing behind a chair in her room, clinging to the back of it as if she thought an earthquake were about to topple her over.

"Mother, don't worry. I'll send them away, whoever it is. Only—if it's Nancy West or Myra Jones, you'd want me to let them in, wouldn't you?"

"Not Myra. No, not Myra."

Did she mean it wasn't Myra or that she didn't want to see Myra? Rebekah wasn't sure. But Mother's hands were white as a china doll's clenching the chair's back. And her own were too dirty for soothing. "Mother! It will be all right. I promise it will be all right. Do you hear that? The dogs are settling down already. So maybe it is Miss Myra."

Mother hunkered over and crept around the chair like a little girl playing hide-and-seek, then slid onto a chair. As Rebekah left, she glanced back to see Mother clap her hands into tight blinders over her eyes, something she did whenever anything was unsettling.

"What are you doing here?" was all she could think to say when she saw Aden Robards standing on the porch looking even taller than she'd remembered. The dogs were literally licking his hands, and she had to admit he must not be very wicked with that kind of reception.

He took off his hat, uncovering thick brown hair streaked gold by the sun. She could see challenge burning in his blue eyes. He leaned slightly toward her. "Sorry to disturb you, uh, Miss Thornton, but I was wondering if your father could be persuaded, for a price of course, to repair my wagon."

"I thought—I sent you to Mr. Jones."

"Oh, you did. But even though I got there very early, just before sunup, Mr. Jones was already in the field. And I was advised by Mrs. Jones to come here. She said Mr. Thornton is the best smithy for miles around."

She didn't miss the hint of accusation in his voice, the implication that she should have told him this instead of sending him to Mr. Jones. Well, didn't they have enough trouble without taking on that of a stranger, too?

"Well. Yes, he is," she said. "But he's not here. And my

mother is—frightened of strangers. I think you should go."
All this time she'd kept her grimy hands behind her, but she
was very conscious that the front of her dress looked as if
she'd been making mud pies. Well, so what if she had? He
could think whatever he pleased.

"When did you say Mr. Thornton would be back?"

"I didn't say. Mr.—uh—I've forgotten your name—" That
was only a ploy, a small stalling tactic. His name actually had
kind of stuck in her head.

"Robards. Aden Robards."

"Mr. Robards, you must go. If you want to see my father,
you can come back this afternoon—"

"Who is it, Rebekah?" Here came Mother sounding strong,
alert even. Now why had she left her room? You could never
tell what she was going to do next.

"You have to go!" Rebekah said, putting her hands out as
if she would push Aden off the porch.

He stepped back and let out a low whistle, then grinned as
he pointed at her dirty hands. "A gardener, aren't you?"

She grimaced before shoving her hands behind her again.

"Why don't you let the young man stay, Honey? He looks
harmless enough. What did he say he wants?" Phoebe
Thornton leaned her tiny frame against Rebekah, then pulled
back, wrinkling her nose at the scent of earth and onions.

"He wants a blacksmith, Mother. He wants someone to
mend his wagon wheel. But you know Father's not here—"

"Oh, he'll be back in a butter dash—don't you worry.
Come in, young man—no need for you to leave and come
again. My daughter's forgotten her manners. We've kept her
so busy, she hasn't had many beaus. And it's time that started
happening, Child. It certainly is."

Rebekah directed significant looks toward Aden, hoping
he'd get the message that Mother wasn't quite well, but his
mischievous crooked grin didn't relieve the heat in her face.
And now that Mother was determined to do so, there was

nothing for her to do but to invite this most irritating man into the house. Mother even suggested that he sit and talk with her while Rebekah prepared some dinner. And there was no telling under the sun what all she might tell him while Rebekah was out of the room. But going against her mother's wishes would cause more trouble than anything, so she complied.

After scrubbing herself, changing into her blue dress, and tying on a white apron, Rebekah went to work making corn pones and frying fatback. If that imposter didn't like the menu, it was too bad. She hoped Father would come back soon, take care of the man, and send him on his way.

Mr. Thornton did get home in time for the noonday meal, and, though he was surprised to find Aden Robards there, Rebekah noticed his worry wrinkles relaxing, his eyes brightening as he and Aden chatted. By the time they had the blessing and were beginning to eat, Father had progressed to asking Aden about his use of ether and his method of filling cavities.

"I don't fill a lot of cavities. Mostly pull teeth. And I don't use ether a lot. It's according to how bad the case is. Now when I was pulling old Hank Jordan's molars, knowing he had his shotgun propped against a tree only six feet away, I decided it was wise to make him a little bit happy. That was up in North Carolina, I think."

Mr. Thornton's laughter invited more examples of dentistry from Aden, who was able to consume pone after pone while he talked.

Phoebe Thornton fidgeted in her chair as the conversation developed into less than pleasant images, even gory details. Maybe her uneasiness had nothing to do with the topic at hand, but Rebekah cleared her throat and gave Father a hard look, then finally suggested she didn't think Mother was enjoying the toothy descriptions. Aden now shook with laughter.

"I do apologize, Mrs. Thornton," said Aden when he could recover his voice. "It was downright thoughtless of me. I talk about these things so much, I forget sometimes where I am and who's listening."

Rebekah watched his face to see if the edgy look came into his eyes as it came to everyone nowadays when they talked to Mother's blank stare. But instead he kept his gaze directed steadily toward Mother's face until he'd finished his apology; then he turned a beaming smile on Rebekah as he reached for yet more corn pones.

Father grunted his disapproval of the ladies having demolished a perfectly good conversation. "Well," he said, "maybe it wouldn't offend anyone, including you, if I ask where you went to school, Dr. Robards?"

"Please. Just call me Aden. I attended Fletcher's Dental School in New York for a couple of years, then studied with a dentist for a year. Many itinerant dentists decide to pull teeth, acquire a few basic instruments, and begin without a whit of schooling. They sort of spoil the reputation of the profession. I wanted to do the right thing, to be prepared as much as possible. But I confess I became impatient—wanted to get on out and get to work."

Father nodded. "I can understand that. You wanted to be out on your own."

Aden placed his elbows on the table and hunched forward, his face eager with a further explanation. "The dentist I was apprenticed to—well, the man knew his jawbones, but he had no gentleness to go with it. The business was more important to him than relieving pain, so he turned folks away because they couldn't pay. I couldn't live with that. So here I am a year later learning more with every patient. I mean to be very careful, of course, about how I tackle problems outside my expertise."

Mr. Thornton chuckled. "I notice you said you're careful about how you attempt to solve problems, not that you won't. You needn't be apologetic around here, Son. We don't have a dentist near here to be upset or jealous of your prac-

ticing. And most of us, when we need a tooth pulled, get a
friend or neighbor to fetch his pliers. Beyond that help, we
usually tie herbs on our swollen jaws and keep working.
Now we used to have a man here, a Harvard graduate, wasn't
he, Rebekah? He sure did let everybody know he was an
authority. Folks didn't care too much for his ways. Called
him uppity. But—there must be more to your deciding to
travel so far. Seems mighty lonesome to me."

Aden accepted a cup of coffee from Rebekah and stirred in
some cream and sugar before answering. "My mother thought
so, too. And there is more. I really felt—feel—God wants me
to do this, to go from town to town relieving a pain here and
there. Pain—just pain alone—" He paused and tapped his
spoon gently against the rim of his cup. "Pain takes away so
much joy. You'll probably think this is crazy, but there's a verse
in Isaiah—chapter fifty-eight, verse twelve, to be exact—that
says, 'And thou shalt be called the repairer of the breach, the
restorer of paths to dwell in.' I'm a repairer of the breach; at
least that's what I'd like to be! And not just breaches in teeth
but in lives. You'd be amazed at how many opportunities I have
to tell people about eternal life while their mouths are agape."

"You don't say!" Mr. Thornton slapped his hand on the
table and let his laughter roll, though Rebekah was having
trouble seeing anything funny. All that about repairing
breaches sounded positively arrogant to her. Mrs. Thornton
turned a startled face toward her laughing husband, then put
both hands hard over her eyes. Mr. Thornton lowered his
voice.

"About that wagon wheel—" Rebekah reminded them.

"Oh, that's right—you have a broken wheel. I should be
able to help you," said Mr. Thornton, sopping a last dribble
of sorghum with a bite of corn pone before pushing his chair
back.

Rebekah watched Aden stoop as he followed Father through
the low door leading from the kitchen to the dogtrot hallway.

One would think they'd been friends forever instead of only a few hours the way they chatted on and on. And why should that be irksome to her? Maybe because Father was enjoying himself and she was so miserable. How could Father be jovial at a time like this, when Thornapple was about to be snatched from them? And somehow, if only because he'd appeared on the scene just at this time, this talkative dentist seemed partially responsible for all that was happening. Oh, she knew he wasn't even aware of their problems. But if only he'd stayed out of their lives right now, maybe Father could concentrate well enough to figure out some strategy for saving the farm.

While she was staring after them, Aden suddenly popped back in. A wide grin split his tanned face as he set his right forearm across his middle and bowed from the waist. "Thank you for a very good meal, mesdames," he said.

Again, Rebekah noticed, Aden spoke to each of them directly, his face registering no problem with the emptiness in Mother's gaze. She certainly had to admit he was good with Mother. Would Aunt Constance be able to treat Mother as respectfully as this stranger had done?

❧

When Mr. Thornton examined the wagon wheel, pursing his lips in thought, he mumbled to himself about how he would make repairs. Finally he straightened, gave his nose a vigorous rubbing, then studied Aden's face intently until Aden reddened under his scrutiny. "Probably take me a couple of days to get this for you. You could stick around here, I reckon. Eat with us, sleep in our barn or in your wagon, whichever you like. Maybe even pull a few teeth if word gets out you're here."

Aden's heart leaped. This arrangement was too perfect! A place for him and his horses in the barn, solid good meals every day, permission to practice dentistry where his wagon sat—and time to observe Rebekah with her long, shining braid and full, firm lips.

When the wheel repairs were complete and the two men had the wagon ready to roll, Mr. Thornton observed that Aden's horses were in need of shoeing. "You'd best stay around a while longer, Son. Let me help you out here. How many miles these horses come by now?"

"Oh, well, let's see—I figured out a while back it might be a thousand or more. But you know they get to rest while I'm working. They need to be reshod, hmm? It has been a long time since that smithy in—Virginia, I think, Shenandoah Valley—put them on while I saw to his family's teeth."

"Now that sounds like a winner. You could do that for us. Except"—Mr. Thornton pulled at his mustache and walked around Jolly as if he were thinking more about feet than teeth—"my ladies aren't going to be too keen on your knocking about in their mouths. My wife—well, I guess you've noticed—she's got some kind of difficulty. I guess you'd say she's kind of left us so far as her mind's concerned, but her body's still here. Doctors can't do a thing. And my daughter. Rebekah. Well, she's as stubborn as General Lee ever thought about being. Reminds me of a general sometimes, too," he added with a grin.

"How's that, Sir?" prodded Aden, thoroughly enjoying these insights.

"She'd rather give orders than take them. Anyway, though, her teeth—"

"Everyone could use some dental assistance from time to time," said Aden cheerfully. "I'd be glad to take a look."

Mr. Thornton studied Aden's face, and a twinkle came into his blue eyes. "It wouldn't hurt to try," he said finally.

"So it's a deal? You shoe my horses and I give you dental assistance? Even swap?"

"Even swap, including wheel repairs," said Mr. Thornton, offering his hand in a confirming shake. "But remember— we can't approach Mrs. Thornton with this. You can do double work in my mouth. I'd be glad if you'd try some of those fillings on some of these teeth so I can save them for awhile. I kind of like my teeth, you know."

Mr. Thornton was right about Rebekah. No one was touching her teeth. They'd have had to tie her to a chair and hold an ether rag over her nose to get a chance even to look in her mouth. Aden quickly realized his powers of persuasion fell far short in her case. But he wouldn't be beaten completely. "Perhaps another time," he said with one of his big, flashing smiles.

Rebekah grimaced as she shook her head. "Not ever, thank you."

But if Rebekah wanted no part of the dentist's help, her neighbors were just the opposite. As soon as the word was out that a dentist had set up over at Thornapple, people began to come by twos and threes and families.

Not only did neighbors come for dental help, but many of them, even neighbors who hadn't been to Thornapple for a long time, not since Phoebe Thornton began "acting funny," now came in the evenings to visit. Whether their motivation was from fascination with the visiting dentist and his tales or sympathy for the Thorntons themselves in their difficulties, they'd sit long hours on the porch. Subjects of conversation ranged from plans for Atlanta's Cotton Exposition in the fall to the price they could expect per bushel of corn and per bale of cotton and how well everyone's chickens were laying. With so many people coming and going, sometimes Mrs. Thornton would not budge from her room; other times she would peer from a front window like a little pinch-faced ghost. But often Rebekah or Myra Jones or Nancy West would persuade her at least to be present for fun on the porch, even if all she did was to sit wrapped in a shawl in her rocking chair.

Aden, always alert to what Rebekah might be doing or saying, noticed that two, or even three, young men were trying to be more than friends to her. He watched her diligently from the corners of his eyes whether he was listening to Mr. Jones describe advantages of diversity in field crops or whether he himself was telling one of his travel tales. He was convinced she didn't care for any of her suitors, but he wasn't sure that was a very good sign for him.

One night he told a story about three elderly sisters who decided to have their teeth pulled so they could have nice white smiles, supposing of course they could have false teeth installed. At just the time he was beginning to describe the anger they displayed when he refused to pull any of their teeth, he looked around and realized Rebekah was gone. As he talked, he searched the shadows for her slim figure. He couldn't cheat his audience. They'd invested time in this story, and he must finish it no matter how distracted he was. Had Rebekah drifted out of hearing to go talk to her horse or watch the sunset from Monarch Mountain—and was she alone? And what on earth could he do about it anyway?

Farmers leaning against porch posts or sitting on steps were hunched his direction in expectation. Their wives occupying chairs and stools or pacing with babies on hips giggled as if they weren't sure whether to laugh at the ladies wanting new teeth or to commiserate with them. He'd not disappoint any of them. But by the time he got to the part where the frustrated women told lies on him until he had to leave town in the middle of the night, he was hardly conscious of the cries of dismay that rose from the porch sitters. He responded to them, assuring them he hadn't minded that much, that it was time for him to move on anyway, and that the way he saw it, if he made decisions he thought God would like, he'd be all right even if he landed in jail. But, though he responded, later in his bedroll in the barn he couldn't remember what he'd said. Had he even made any sense?

What was he going to do? Time was running out. He'd be leaving, and the family was moving away. If he left now, would he ever see Rebekah again and especially before she became someone else's wife? He talked to God each day about it. "I don't mean to be impatient, Father, but You know if this is what You want for me, You've got to show me what to do to win this girl on such short notice." It seemed to him the more he paid attention to her, the more irritable she became. And no matter how he tried, he couldn't bring a sparkle to her eyes.

❧

Rebekah confided in the Talking Tree one day. "It's as if everyone's forgotten what's happening to the farm. That big stranger has captured their attention, and I don't know why. He talks too much, he's far too handsome for his own good even if he doesn't shave often enough, and I don't like him. But he's won Father over so completely he's acting as if all's well. Oh, Tree, I feel as if—I'm a leaf in a stream about to hit a rapids. And I'm so, so scared." She sat cupped between great roots at the pine's base with her knees pulled up under her chin, watching sun circles flicker and dance in a rhythmic ever-changing shadow pattern on Tree's personal straw carpet. Why, why couldn't things stay the same for any longer? If only she could press this scene, wind and all, between the pages of a favorite book. If only she could hold onto Thornapple! What could Josh have been thinking? Well, Father said Josh was remorseful now. But the damage was done.

Rebekah took several trips into town on the excuse of telling this one or that one about dental opportunities when really her main reason was to seek employment. Perhaps she could appease the bank with some small payments if she could figure out how to generate some cash. But her efforts met with sympathetic nods, sometimes lowered eyelids, when old family acquaintances had to say no. No one needed any service she could offer.

One day as Rebekah and her father sorted tools and equipment in the barn, he broached the subject of her future, suggesting strongly that she accept a proposal of marriage. It looked as if, he pointed out, she had a good choice between Oliver Lightfoot and John Burbank, that both seemed mighty fine young men and very fond of her. Rebekah exploded. She was married to Thornapple, and she wanted no other marriage.

"Rebekah, don't—don't make it so hard," said her father. "Girl, you need someone to share your life with, and it would sure help us all if you could make a decision pretty soon. Because the worst of all this is leaving you stranded. If Constance weren't so ornery, I'd—"

"I'm not stranded, Father. You said Mr. Jones agreed for me to stay there, remember? Now stop trying to marry me off! I'll make my own arrangements." She plunked a rusty wrench into a wooden box of small tools and bit her lip as she yanked at a snarl of wire. "You need to spend more time worrying about taking care of Mother. You'll have to be extremely patient with her, Father, her moving away from all that's familiar and all. And don't—don't let Aunt Constance badger her. Please—take good care of her."

"I will. I will!" Rebekah knew her father well enough to be sure the irritation in his voice meant he didn't like this traumatic change any more than she did. But why didn't he figure out some alternative if he didn't like it?

Rebekah began wrestling the wire into some kind of order. If she wound this wire quickly and tightly enough, maybe she'd smother her pain. Father had no idea how very much she dreaded staying with the Joneses. She had almost nothing in common with those girls who worked as little as possible and spent the rest of their time perfecting their hair, skin, and nails. All three girls played the piano, and for that Rebekah envied them, but it was the only thing she envied them for, at least until now. Now she envied their being able to keep their farm. Well, she would work on their farm to earn her keep, and she would stay there no longer than it took to figure out something else.

And the "something else" wouldn't be marriage. *Oliver*

Lightfoot and John Burbank indeed, Rebekah scoffed to herself. Why, she'd as soon marry that traveling dentist as either one of those stodgy fellows.

Maybe it was that outlandish thought that kept her from turning Aden down when he invited her to go walking with him one afternoon. She had plenty of excuses not to go, but somehow when she tried them out, they sounded pretty lame. Next thing she knew she was hooking her apron over a chair post and walking out the door with him. After all, this wouldn't take long.

They walked down Thornapple's road with the dogs zigzagging merrily from one side to the other, scouting for rabbits and field mice. Shadows of oak and pine lay across the sandy ruts with leaf patterns shifting in the barest breath of a breeze. They talked about the weather, the dogs, and the horses. Not too much to argue about on those subjects. Rebekah began to relax. They'd soon turn around and head back to the house.

Aden cleared his throat. "I need to ask you something. Don't say no before you've thought about it. It's very important. Promise?"

"I don't make promises about anything I don't understand," she said. "But ask anyway."

"I want you to marry me," he said as calmly, as if he said it every day.

"What did you say?" She must have heard him wrong.

"I said I want you to marry me."

"No!" she answered with spirit, turning toward him as she knotted folds of her skirt in her hands. Seeing the amusement twitching at a corner of his mouth and twinkling in his eyes angered her even more. "How dare you be so presumptuous!"

"Hey, I said don't say no before you've thought," he reminded her in a gentle reprimand. "Every question deserves a contemplative answer."

She wanted to slap the silly grin off his face. But instead

she swallowed hard and started walking quickly.

"Why would you want to marry me?" she asked, wishing her voice wouldn't shake. "You can tell I don't love you, and you know the last thing I want to do is leave Thornapple."

"My understanding is you'll have to leave no matter what you want. You'll have to go somewhere. Why not with me?"

"Marrying someone because there's nothing else to do is not what I had expected," said Rebekah.

"No. But for eons people have married because it was a good match and have learned to love each other. I think—I believe it can happen for us." Was that a wistful note in his voice? Rebekah noticed with a sidelong glance that his hands were clenched at his sides. He was actually serious!

"I don't see how you think we're a good match. I love this farm and want to stay right here. I'm a good farmer myself, not just a farmer's daughter. And you—you will always want to move, I guess. Anyway—I never intended to marry anyone at all, and certainly not like—not like this." Rebekah's face felt hot, and she was as uncomfortable all over as if she'd rolled in a patch of nettles. Suddenly she couldn't bear to continue this unbelievable conversation. Lifting her skirts to her ankles, she fled toward the house without a backward glance.

⇌

Aden turned and watched her go. Soon he heard the splatter of Firefly's hoofbeats heading toward the back of Thornapple. If only he had more time, he could court her as slowly as she deserved!

⇌

It was on the day of the estate sale that she said yes.

Plowshare, hay sweep, harrow, foot-pedaled grinding stone, and even her broken hoe were all laid out under the oaks with eager strangers and sad neighbors picking over them. Chairs, table, her dresser and mirror with its mottled designs of Virginia and the Atlantic Ocean, a sideboard, the big wooden bread bowl—the very bones of their daily lives were on display on the porch and under the trees for the perusal of buyers.

She couldn't bear these depressing scenes one minute more. She'd go to her garden. There she found tiny green points of onion plants thrusting upward, but she wouldn't allow herself to kneel and touch one shoot. They were not hers! Turning away, she stumbled to the well house. Leaning her forehead hard against a post, she gripped splintery wood.

The sound of footsteps behind her gave her the resolve she needed to hold back her sobs.

"Say yes, Rebekah," said Aden quietly. "You can't stay here, you know, and I—I would take good care of you."

"Why does it make any difference to you what happens to me?" She tried not to let her anger show. Why should she be angry with him? It wasn't his fault all this was happening.

"Because I care. I just do. I—Rebekah, I *need* you for my wife."

"Cook, washerwoman, such as that?"

"More than that. Listen. There's something I haven't told you. Maybe it won't mean much to you now, but I have to tell you. You see, my whole name is Isaac Aden Robards. Remember Isaac and Rebekah in the Bible?"

"Yes. Abraham sent for a wife for his son, Isaac, and the servant brought back Rebekah. I never understood how Rebekah could leave her home and go with a stranger that way. It didn't make a bit of sense."

"No. I guess it didn't," he said. "Because you haven't learned yet about following God's leadings."

"And what is that supposed to mean? That I'm not spiritual enough?"

"We all have room to grow, don't we?" he asked.

"Well. Sure. But what do our names have to do with this? Surely you don't think—I mean this is 1881 in Georgia not 'whatever' B.C. in the Promised Land. And anyway, you're Isaac yourself. If you wanted to do a reenactment, you should have sent your servant. Or is there a hidden master somewhere? Are you really the servant?"

"Please don't laugh. Although I guess it does sound pretty funny. But I'm absolutely serious about this. And I'm not trying to stage a reenactment. I know the analogy isn't complete. This is what's happened. God has shown me He'd give me a wife and I'd know who it is because, aside from His telling me in my heart, her name would be Rebekah."

Rebekah put her hand to her mouth. "You can't make decisions based on—"

"A word from the Lord? Absolutely. It's the safest way of doing business, simply obeying the Lord."

"Oh. So this is business, is it?" She hoped the sudden wave of bitterness didn't come out in her voice.

"I didn't mean that." He spread his hands at his sides and stepped toward her, then hooked his thumbs in his pockets as he looked down at her, his blue eyes darkened by the well-house shadow. "I did not mean that," he said again.

Rebekah hardened her chin and straightened her back as she came to a decision. "Well, maybe you don't think of it as business, but I do. If you want a wife just to keep house—or, excuse me, wagon—for you, then—all right. I'll go. But I'll only be a cook and washerwoman in reality and if—"

He was looking at her in such solemnity, it was frightening, and she almost forgot what she was saying. She hugged herself. "That's the only way I'll go with you," she said.

He cleared his throat, shoved his hands in his pockets, and looked away from her across fields still lying in wait for seeds. When he turned back, he drew a deep breath and gazed right into her eyes as if reading her inside and out. She found herself actually hoping now he wouldn't change his mind. Maybe this wasn't the marriage Father had in mind, but he couldn't argue much since he'd made such a to-do over this man. The arrangement would solve the present question of "what to do with Rebekah." She'd be taken care of, even if in a rustic manner. And she'd worry about the future later—maybe even still find some way of buying back Thornapple.

"All right then," he said. "I agree to—what you've asked. I'll sleep under the wagon. You can have the inside. But I don't promise not to try to change your mind."

She blushed. "And we'll just—I mean—we will be—"

A nerve jerked in his hardened jaw. "I agree to a marriage of convenience if that's what it's called. For now. That's all I'm agreeing to."

The wedding took place on the porch the very next evening.

four

Dearest Mother,

I hope this finds you well. I'm glad Mr. Arrington has agreed to help you with the orchard. Even though I know I'm where I need to be, I long to be with you, too, tending the trees, pruning, carting, fertilizing, getting ready for the next season. Well, I guess the trees will be abloom soon or are already. It's hard to believe it's full spring again. Almost a year has gone by since I left you to come south.

I know this is going to hurt you, but I can't think of a right way to tell you. Rebekah and I were married on her front porch two weeks ago. It all happened so fast I didn't have time to let you know. Then every day was so full until by and by I found myself feeling that you knew anyway. You, my dear mother, who've been my friend and mentor even before Dad died, would have to know something as amazing as her son's taking a wife. This morning I realized you couldn't possibly know and determined today would be the day I'd write to you.

Rebekah is beautiful. She has long, very long, dark brown hair, which she wears in a single braid down her back. She grew up on a farm near Hogansville, Georgia. Unfortunately, because of her only brother's poor judgment and unwise choices, her family is losing the farm. That grieves Rebekah quite much. I hope I'll be able to make her happy, but sometimes I wonder if I've made a very grave error in the sight of God.

39

Rebekah has already been able to help me with simple dental hygiene jobs and has learned the different instruments, so she's quite handy to have nearby. If only she would smile more! She loves horses, and I mean one day to find her a horse she can love as much as the one she lost in the estate turnover. The reason I said perhaps I'd made a grave error is that Rebekah does not yet love me. I was naive enough to believe she would very soon, since I loved her right from the very moment I first saw her. I didn't have the option of courting her at length because we wouldn't be anywhere near each other. I thought I had to make her my wife and she would soon return my love. It has only been a short time, so I'm sure that will still happen.

Rebekah's parents are living now with Mrs. Thornton's sister in LaGrange. We could have arranged our dental route to include LaGrange but haven't. Will you be shocked if I tell you that I hoped by keeping Rebekah to myself I might get through to her heart? Now we've traveled too far from LaGrange to be going anytime soon. And now that I see how very homesick she is, her face actually pinched with pain, I wish I'd not been so selfish.

We are camping between Cordele and Macon. I like the small towns the best so we probably won't actually practice in Macon but just go in for supplies and mail. I can hear you right now wondering why I'm making such a hard life for my bride as we camp in different places for several nights in a row before we settle on one where I can find plenty of people with dental needs. Rebekah is a very strong and hearty (is it hearty or hardy? I've never been sure!) woman. The camping itself is not something she complains about. Actually, complaining is not one of her faults. She simply doesn't talk. She does her work, whatever I ask her and more, then disappears on long walks or goes to sit under whatever tree she *feels drawn to. The camping chores are light compared to the work she did at Thornapple. I really think the work is all that makes her happy right now.*

All that I've told you is only so you will pray for us. I felt very strongly, more strongly than I ever have about anything, that God wanted me to marry Rebekah. I know God is going to work miracles in our lives and that she soon will begin to return my love. So don't you go to worrying, little Mother. Just pray.

Tell Mr. Arrington please to take special pains with the apple trees in the little valley where that rock juts up high as a horse's head. Those apples, whose name I can't remember, are the sweetest and crispest of all. I can just smell an apple now as if I'd this moment bitten into it.

You can write me in care of General Delivery at Macon. I'll be in the vicinity for several weeks.

> *Love always, your son,*
> *Isaac Aden Robards*

P.S. I talked to one of my clients yesterday about where he expected to spend eternity. He said he was afraid it wouldn't be heaven. He's coming to talk again today! What an opportunity!

"Come now—please get back in the wagon," called Aden over his shoulder to Rebekah, who plodded along half a wagon length behind. "You've got to be tired. And anyway I need to speed up. It's getting late, and we'll have to make camp soon."

The dusty *clip-clop* of horses' hooves was his only answer. Glancing back again, he noted that Rebekah had let her hat slide off so it hung by its string around her neck. Her face had reddened with heat, and she held her left hand against her side as if something were painful.

He slowed to a halt, speaking to the horses softly all the time. But he only watched from the corner of his vision to see Rebekah climb up to her seat beside him. She obviously did not want any attention, so he would try his best to ignore her.

∂∞

Rebekah squirmed on the hard seat. It had been such a long day. She had wanted to walk much more than Aden had agreed to, but now she actually was tired and glad to be back on her seat. Somehow the seat had grown harder while she was out of it. No matter how she shifted, it wasn't comfortable.

She held her hands clasped in a knot in her lap as she watched a family bent in various aching poses over their hoes in a cornfield. A little girl raised her head, then waved at her. She waved back and could tell from the little girl's response that Aden, too, had waved. Farther along, a boy scrubbed his dog in a washtub while three smaller children looked on. Beyond their plain, shedlike house, a man and woman hoed cotton, the man flapping his hat at the passing wagon, the woman never lifting her head. Rebekah wondered how many wagons passed there that the woman could resist looking when one came by. Then she remembered her own hoeing and reflected she might have done the same. How thrilling it had always been to look back along a row of little soldierlike plants and see them neat and free of weeds! Her hands itched to be out there helping the woman. Or, better still, back at Thornapple. The thought of Thornapple without them, the house quiet or occupied by strangers, almost choked her. She put a hand to her mouth and pushed her lip hard against her teeth as she squeezed her eyes shut to discourage a crowding of tears.

"Maybe we're coming to a town soon," said Aden. "I see smoke against the sky. Next farm we'll stop and ask. Maybe they'll offer us a spot to camp. I'd relish some stewed meat tonight, wouldn't you?"

She couldn't answer just now. She would not speak until she knew her voice wouldn't quiver.

"Rebekah?"

She swallowed hard and dashed a hand across her nose as if, she hoped, she were swatting at pesky gnats.

"Stewed meat? We don't have any meat to stew." There! He wanted conversation; she'd give him conversation. She could feel him studying her.

"I'll snag us a rabbit."

"How? You don't have a gun, and it'd take hours to trap one. Even if you had a trap."

A huge grin crept over Aden's face, danced in his blue eyes.

"A bow and arrow will do the trick. You don't believe me, do you?"

"No. No, I don't. By the time you get an arrow in the bow, your rabbit will be half a forest away." She squared her shoulders and lifted her chin.

"Ah. You disappoint me, Lady. You greatly underestimate my speed. Be setting your taste buds for rabbit stew this very night."

She put a hand to her mouth, this time to hide a smile. "I hope you have plenty of arrows."

"Won't take more than one. I'm quick. Quicker than—"

"Lightning?"

"I was going to say quicker than a silver fox chasing this year's spring chicken. But then the best simile would be that I'm quicker than a rabbit." He chuckled.

"Speed is only half of it. Accuracy is just as important," she said.

"I like it when you talk," he said with such open sincerity she immediately felt guilty somehow. Guilty? Why should she feel guilty? She'd done nothing. It was he who had ridden into her life and swept her away from all she loved. *Oh, Rebekah, stop whining. You said yes of your own free will.*

She took a deep breath and slid a peep out from under her

eyelids. He was looking at the road ahead, still grinning, probably picturing himself catching that rabbit. Well, let him enjoy it while he could. He'd certainly not be able to do such a thing, and somehow it would be a comfort to her to see him defeated for once. He was so confident all the time, seemed to believe he could pray anything into reality.

The last three weeks since they'd said their vows on Thornapple's porch had been the worst weeks of Rebekah's life. That first night, though Aden told her the wagon was hers and never once gave her any reason to doubt him, she doubted him anyway. She lay awake all night afraid even to cry for fear he'd hear her and try to comfort her—and more. She hated herself for agreeing to this crazy marriage, and she hated him more for proposing it. Each night she rested easier, but she knew she couldn't trust this man. Why should she? He couldn't have married her for love any more than she had him. And no matter what he'd said his reason was, she really didn't know.

She should have stayed with the Joneses as Father had meant for her to. She'd at least have been able to keep a nearby watch on Thornapple's progress. Or she should have gone with Father and Mother to Aunt Constance's. What loyal daughter would let her parents go off like that without even a fight? How were they doing now? Was Aunt Constance bossing Father and fussing over Mother till they were both going mad? It really was inconceivable that they could be getting along very well without her. They never had before in her whole life.

Aden hauled on the reins at a crossing, eyed the sun, then traveled straight ahead. He pointed to a modest, two-story house with high steps. "That's the farm we've been looking for," he said. "Not that I know the folks. I just think they'll give us a place to camp." No sooner had he pulled off the main road onto the rutted, jerky little lane than people began popping out all sides of the house and running from a nearby barn. Children even scrambled out from under the house where, by the looks of their faces, they must have been making mud pies.

The children, each with cotton-blond hair cut as if around a bowl, stared silently at Rebekah from afar, while Aden talked to a man dressed in overalls with gaping holes in both knees.

"We have permission to camp," announced Aden, returning to the wagon.

"Where are we?" she asked, sliding down without using Aden's offered hand.

"Oh, about thirty miles from Macon still," he said. "There's a small town nearby. They haven't had a dentist through here in over a year. Mr. Sharp says he thinks we should stay right here. Well, in the bottom beyond that rise. Says he can bring plenty of clients to us, as many as we can take care of."

In spite of herself, she warmed to his use of the pronoun "we." It felt good, his including her in the work. She'd felt like such a clumsy, useless bump while she tried to learn his movements and know the instruments and when he would need them. She'd felt a horrible revulsion when trying to hold slimy tongues out of the way, had once or twice worried that she'd throw up in the middle of a dental procedure. But she thought she was past that, and he must think so, too, to include her as part of the team. Still, she wasn't ready to show any enthusiasm for his work so, not knowing what to say, she said nothing. Walking quickly, she followed the creaking wagon up a gentle slope, very glad to make this short stint on foot.

"Evenin', Ma'am," said a woman standing close to the rutted path. She held one blond-headed baby close to her thick body while a slightly older one clung to her skirts sucking its thumb. "How do you do?"

"Oh, hello. I'm—I'm glad you can let us stay. Uh-mm. My name's Rebekah."

"Amanda's my name. And that's my husband, Idus. This here's my two babies. Rest of the children you seen gawkin' at you is now a-hidin', I reckin. We don't see company too much. Anyways, don't—don't hold back from comin' fer help anytime, you hear?"

"Thank you. Thank you very much," said Rebekah, feeling a warm flash of comfort just knowing this stranger genuinely cared. She had so many to care for already.

The man named Idus strode ahead of the wagon carrying an ax. Halfway down the hill, he yelled back over his shoulder for his wife to set Tom to work milking the cows. "An' tell 'im I'll wring his ever-lovin' neck if he wastes that there feed this time," he said before saying something to Aden about where his horses could graze.

Rebekah looked back and saw Amanda Sharp scooting toward the house looking for all the world like a mother hen with her brood. She was obviously intimidated by the long-legged, long-faced, stern-voiced Idus Sharp. Pretty appropriate name the man had.

Mr. Sharp had already begun trimming sprouts and underbrush out of the way by the time Rebekah reached their new campsite. He gave Aden instructions about boundaries for the horses and which trees were all right for firewood. Rebekah tried to add her own thank-you to Aden's when Mr. Sharp prepared to leave, but she could never get a word in edgewise or even catch his eye. The man was focused all right. As he strode away, his ax slung over his shoulder, she couldn't help wondering what little round Amanda Sharp had seen in this stern, grizzly man to marry him. Then she chuckled out loud.

"What is it?" asked Aden, looking up from where he struggled to level the wagon.

"Nothing," she declared. She couldn't explain to him that she found it funny that she, who had landed in such a very odd marriage, should even think of criticizing anyone else for their choice.

As soon as the horses were watered and fed, Aden unhooked his bow and arrow from one side of the wagon and threw her a crooked grin as he prepared to leave camp. "I won't be long," he said. "It's kinda cloudy, and it's getting late. Rabbits will be out for their evening nibbles. Don't suppose— you could build a fire while I'm gone?"

"Of course I can!" she answered with more confidence than she felt. She was prepared to defend her eligibility as fire builder but realized Aden didn't really care. He was already ambling out of camp, testing the flexibility of his bow as he went.

Rebekah tossed her braid over her shoulder as she placed her hands on her hips and turned slowly, surveying her situation. The horses munched their grain nearby; a stream murmured not far away. A pair of blue jays squawked at each other in a hickory tree. Mr. Sharp had laid a few dry sticks together in the spot he'd recommended as good for a campfire. But it wouldn't be enough. She'd have to scout out some more before she could begin to make a merry, lasting blaze. She needed to stir quickly if she didn't want to be ashamed when Aden returned. But she hugged herself instead, leaning her head back and taking in a deep breath of the woodsy smells. Freedom! She was actually alone with no one in sight from any direction. That had happened so seldom lately. Oh, she knew the plain little farmhouse was over the hill, but she couldn't see it. And she knew that not far away Aden was slipping through the woods like a dark shadow, but she couldn't see him either. She was alone!

She found a pile of dry limbs not far down the creek where a tree had been cut. She broke and wrestled out several likely sticks and hauled them to camp. "Thirty miles from Macon," Aden had said. She could walk thirty miles in only a day or two, she was sure. And she knew some cousins in Macon who might help her. Now would be a good time to go while Aden was out trying to get that rabbit. When he came hunting for her, she could easily hide and was sure she could elude him. But she continued setting a fire, even stuffed light sticks and leaves under the pyramid she'd created before plundering in the wagon for Aden's precious box of matches. It didn't seem like a wise move right now to walk off and leave him. Oh, she knew he'd be fine without her—better, she supposed. But whether a dumb promise or not, she had made a commitment, and she wasn't ready yet to break it. He had been good to give her an alternative to being a charity case at the Joneses'. Not that she wanted to admit that, but it was true. And perhaps her pride rebelled at the thought of admitting to distant cousins that her father had lost the farm, that they were all penniless now because Josh had been so stupid. She much preferred to think that in six months somehow she'd have at least a small fund to help her go home to Thornapple and begin again, however humbly.

She still hadn't found Aden's matches or his flint.

She looked under his wagon seat where she'd seen him tuck things before but couldn't find anything except books and papers and a picture of his mother. "She looks sweet," she mused, sliding it back under the seat much more carefully than she had pulled it out.

She searched Aden's medicine bag and his instrument chest with empty results. He was going to be back soon and would certainly laugh at her for not having a fire. But he hadn't told her where the matches were, and how was she supposed to know? She investigated a cache of various and sundry items stored in an upside-down table and wondered why in the world Aden was hauling this fancy little table around with him. Must belong to his mother. But, no, she wouldn't give him something like that when he was going off to live in a wagon. She shrugged and turned to the next corner.

Steeling herself, she plunged her hand into the pockets of Aden's spare pair of brown pants, roughly folded by the wagon's back opening. Still nothing. Feeling along the edge of the wagon, her hands touched a metal box. Surely he didn't keep them in the cash box! Her hand rested on the cool, closed box. Her heart rate accelerated even more than it had when she touched his clothes and other personal articles. This was very private, and she knew it. Anyway it would be locked.

She held her breath as she tried the lid. It opened without a sound. She felt inside and stifled a gasp, then glanced behind her at the dim twilight outside. The box was full of money! How had Aden ever saved up that much from just pulling and filling teeth? Especially when so often he took potatoes or eggs or a pound of lard for his pay.

A joyful shout outside made Rebekah close the lid and scramble for the wagon's opening. Aden stood there holding a rabbit by its hind legs, his face even in the dusky light a picture of pride and triumph.

"Isn't it a beauty now?" he exclaimed, shaking the rabbit, bloody head dangling, entirely too close to her face.

She put a hand over her mouth at the fresh-killed smell. "Don't! I—uh—"

"Hey, now! You a farm girl and still so squeamish? I guess—you're not a typical farm girl, huh? You feel sorry for the poor little thing. Well, I do, too. But it had a good life and now—into the pot! Where's that roaring fire you were going to build?"

A flush crept up her neck. There was no missing the mockery in his voice as he glanced at her pile of sticks.

"I couldn't find your matches or flints either. I'm not a magician, you know."

"Oh. Sorry. My flints are here in my pocket. We're out of matches. Here, use both flints and—well, you know how to do it."

He handed her the flints, then pulled out his knife and sauntered away to dress his rabbit. She rubbed flints together as she'd seen him do. Nothing happened. She rubbed and rubbed some more. Wasn't as easy to achieve sparks as he'd made it appear. He'd known it would be hard. That's why he'd worn that smug smile. What else did he know? Did he know she'd opened his money box? Did he hear the lid shut? Not that it mattered. She hadn't taken anything. And she'd only been looking for his flints. So why did she feel guilty?

Sparks finally flew, and she teased alive a tiny blaze, feeding it with stouter and stouter sticks until it began to lick up the inside of her fine pyramid, and the smell of smoke made her suddenly feel wildly hungry.

"Look! She's done it, Rabbit. She's actually built us a roaring fire!" said Aden in a teasing tone.

"I don't think it's at all proper to talk to a dead rabbit you're about to eat," said Rebekah.

Aden laughed so loudly the horses neighed. "I knew she had some humor in her bones, Rabbit," he said, slapping one knee.

She couldn't help a small chuckle herself. She placed the pot of rabbit covered with water at the edge of the fire. Aden squatted to help her adjust a log to give the pot maximum heat.

They hadn't had much laughter at Thornapple, at least not since Mother had been ill. But before that—had there ever been ringing laughter in those walls? They had been so work-oriented, so serious, all of them. Well, she and Father had joked a little sometimes. Yes, they had. But when Josh was around, it was always tense because he was forever getting into trouble of some kind. Maybe the fact they were so serious caused Josh to look more for fun than anything else at the university. *Do I really have humor in my bones?* she wondered as she turned her head to avoid a puff of smoke.

"I smell rain in the air," observed Aden, casually sniffing the air. "Notice the way the smoke is hanging close, not rising."

"Rain!"

"Yes. You know, moisture that falls in spring and summer as opposed to sleet and snow in winter. Or, as it comes here in the South, pure liquid stuff any time of the year, cold in winter, warm in summer."

She refused to laugh this time at his teasing. Rain! What would they do if it rained?

"Don't you know everywhere we've been it was so terribly dry? It hasn't rained a drop since we left Thornapple."

"I know. But—"

"Well, sooner or later God answers the prayers of the thirsty ground."

"Thirsty ground prays?" She smiled. He could come up with the oddest expressions sometimes.

"Sure. The ground cries out. The birds plead. And people beg."

Rebekah didn't answer. Hadn't she known it would rain eventually? And what did she think was going to happen? Did she think the wagon would magically become a three- or four-room house?

Neither said anything for awhile. Aden whittled a sour-wood stick into a pencil point. Rebekah took out her bag of rag strips and wove them one at a time into a square on a small hand-sized frame. It was something she'd thought to bring from home to help keep her connected with who she was. Sometimes she took out stacks of squares she'd finished and sewed them together in rows. She supposed it would be a rug or a blanket, though she hadn't decided for sure. Right now it was simply a sanity saver.

When the first clap of thunder rolled across the sky, sounding like giants beating on a dozen steel drums, she jumped as if she'd been hit.

"Told you," said Aden. "I guess you do know what happens around here when it rains."

"No. What?" She searched his firelit face, hoping to see that mischievous look. He looked entirely serious.

"Well. You can't expect me to sleep on the ground in the pouring rain."

"You—you can't—"

"I know I can't. You'll have to make room for me inside."

Before Rebekah could think what to say, Aden let out

another big laugh. "You know I wouldn't do that to you, Rebekah. I'm only teasing. Don't you know that?" His laughter gave way quickly to a groan of remorse. "You *know* I wouldn't force you into a situation you didn't want. Have I ever given you reason to fear?"

"No. I—but I didn't know for sure," she answered, her head turned toward the darkness and the sound of horses stirring restlessly.

The stew was tastier than any meat she'd ever put in her mouth. She embarrassed herself by taking more and more. They ate the whole rabbit. Aden, putting the lid on the pot and hanging it high in a gum tree, said they'd have the broth for breakfast.

The first big drops fell while he was checking on the horses.

"Hurry! Into the wagon with you!" he said impatiently when he saw Rebekah was huddled by the spitting fire.

"It's your wagon! It's not fair for me to take cover and leave you in the rain. I—"

"You'll get in the wagon. Now!" Aden grabbed her by the shoulders and lifted her before she could resist. "You'll do exactly as I say for once. Now stay dry and stop worrying!" he said, his voice crackling like lightning itself. He gave her a final shove into the wagon. "Just throw me that old piece of tarp rolled up there in the back."

"You can't sleep out there, Aden! We'll both have to—"

"Throw me the tarp!" he barked.

She wanted to refuse, but the rain was cold and wet, and what was she to do? She longed to be back at Thornapple listening to the storm from her upstairs room. But it was silly and sentimental to think that way. She was here in a stranger's pasture with a man she didn't love who called himself her husband, and all the shelter they had was a silly, small wagon.

five

The rain increased quickly from a sound of spattering on canvas to a mighty roar that drowned out every other sound. She tried to whistle a tune for diversion and could not hear it for the pounding rain and bellowing thunder. Thunder spoke at long intervals, then closer and closer together in angrier and angrier bursts. Lightning illuminated the wagon's interior in heart-stopping whiteness, bleaching the ribbed canvas till it looked like Mother's best linens stretched overhead, then left it darker than before. The air smelled like a struck match in her own room at Thornapple.

She swiped at tears—furtively—as if someone, Aden in particular, might be observing. As the storm became even louder, she tried to distance it by putting a rough wool blanket over her head. The warmth was comforting, and finally she felt herself drifting into sleep in spite of everything. What you couldn't help you just accepted. "Do the best you can and move on," Father always said. *Move on—move on—move on.* She was plowing a straight row, aiming for a tall pine she could sight right between the ears of Father's slow and steady mule Tilley. Suddenly the tree burst into scorching, licking flames that filled her vision. She sat up, breathing hard and clutching her blanket as if she had a death grip on Tilley's plow lines.

Water ran, not in a stream, not in little rivulets, but like a creek splashing under the very wagon. Under the wagon? Aden! He'd be drowned under there! She couldn't let him spend one more minute in this flood.

"Aden!" No sound but the roar of running water. "Aden!" She scrambled toward the opening. The opening wasn't

53

there! In smothering darkness she scrambled to find the heavy curtain flap. There! But beyond the curtain was something else—the tarp? Aden hadn't been sleeping on the tarp; he'd put it over the end of the wagon to protect her! And where was he now?

Suddenly he answered from only inches away, thrusting his head through the wagon flap. "Rebekah! What's wrong?"

"You can't stay out there!" she shouted and then felt his wet hand giving her shoulder a reassuring shake.

"It's okay," he said near her ear, water splashing against her face from his clothes.

"You can't stay out there!" she tried again. "You—you'll drown!"

"I won't drown," he said, but he climbed in anyway. "No need for us both to get wet while we argue. That tarp's not doing a lot of good."

He smelled of wet wool, and the wagon shook as he scrambled in. She crawled back to her own space and hid under her blanket. She thought she should tell him not to sit around wet and catch pneumonia, was working up her nerve, when she became aware that the wagon's continued bouncing must be a result of his struggling into dry things. When she thought he was done, she crawled toward him with an extra blanket. She could only sense his bulk where he sat near the flap.

"Here!" she said, fumbling as she tried to lay the blanket around his shoulders. He didn't respond and seemed to be asleep. She tightened the blanket around him so it would stay put. As she drew back, he suddenly reached out and grasped her hand hard. She was so startled, she forgot to resist. His hand was surprisingly warm for someone who'd been out in a flood. She didn't realize what he was up to until it was too late. In a swift motion, he lifted her hand to his lips and kissed it, his stubbly beard grazing her fingers. She jerked her hand away as if she'd been scalded.

"How dare you?" she screamed.

How could he! How could he? Her heart beat so hard, he probably could hear it even with thunder rumbling like a hungry lion seeking its prey. She pressed her knuckles against her eyes and swallowed hard. She'd simply sit up all night. No matter how religious the man was, he was still a man. She couldn't trust him.

In the early morning half-light Rebekah opened her eyes. A rough edge of her dry wool blanket tickled her cheek. She wiggled her toes as she carefully uncurled herself from a tight knot. What day was it? Where was she? A steady patter of raindrops beat against the canvas top. She sat up in sudden dismay. Aden was right here in the wagon with her. There he sat Indian style, his back to her, his head sunk into his chest. Was he asleep like that?

"It's all right, Rebekah," he said as if he'd heard her very thoughts. "You were kind of snoring so I knew you were asleep. I tossed the extra blanket over you—haphazard-like, you know. I was afraid you were cold."

"What—are you doing? How can you sleep sitting up like that?"

"Oh. It's not really hard. I'm used to it. Besides—"

"What?" she asked.

"I wasn't sleeping all the time. I was praying."

"It was that bad?"

"No, no!" He laughed and turned toward her. His teeth shone white in the dusky interior. "Just a good time to pray. Boy! What a show God put on last night! Like a million stars came down to explode in visitation! Hey, hey! Everything's fine, Rebekah. Don't look so—nervous! Storm's over now. I've already been out checking on the horses. They didn't break tether, and neither of them got struck by lightning. We're in good shape, I'd say."

"We need shelter for them, don't we? Is there—it feels as if we're pretty steady. I mean—I wouldn't have been surprised if we'd floated away."

"Neither would I. You probably would have floated away if you hadn't been kind enough to invite me in. My added weight kept the wagon stationary." He grinned impishly.

"That's the only reason I invited you in, of course," she answered, trying hard not to blush and not being sure whether or not she succeeded. "You could check with Mr. Sharp and see if he has room for your horses in his barn."

"Right. I'll do that. Immediately following breakfast."

"Breakfast? In this rain?"

"Certainly, Madam! Can't afford to starve, you know! Rabbit broth coming right up," he said, sliding out backward, then slipping under the added tarp. "Whooee! What cold rain! Say, that broth is probably watered down perfectly about now—as I will be!"

How in the world would he make a fire in the rain? Maybe the man who'd figured out how to make that piece of added canvas stay put in such a wind could also devise a way to serve warm broth. But he didn't. He made no excuses. Some things were really impossible. He brought her broth so cold it left tallow sticking to her tongue and the roof of her mouth. She couldn't take a second swallow, but he downed his as well as hers and gave her a wide grin. "Delicious!" he declared cheerfully. He was standing on the ground with only his head and shoulders thrust inward through the wagon's tail flap. Setting his cup down to rake water out of his eyes, he then said, "I guess you're right. I'd best go up to the Sharps and see if I can borrow some stall space. Looks as if the rain's settling in to be a long one."

She nodded. Then in answer to his questioning look, she said, "I'll be fine. I'm not afraid of rain."

She listened to him slog off and finally drew a long, deep breath when she could hear nothing but the pelt of raindrops. Now she could figure out how to perform her morning rituals in this downpour.

Aden returned an hour later with a merry shout as he entered the campsite. "Yo, Rebekah! Good news! Room for the horses and for you!"

"For me! In the barn?"

"No, no! In the house!" He was again leaning into the opening under protection of his added tarpaulin. Water streamed from his soaked hair down his cheeks and dripped off his chin and nose. He considered her gravely. "You don't have to be concerned about—well, protocol, or—you know, questions. I simply explained that my wife is new at this camping-out business and doesn't need to endure the harsh weather—might get sick. I, on the other hand, need to stay with my wagon—be sure nothing gets damaged. You'll like the family, Rebekah, all ages of children, every one of them cute as baby foxes."

"Foxes indeed!" She had to scoff at his comparison before she could go on. She wanted right that minute to be stoic, to tough out the situation rather than be installed with strangers. But she had to think of Aden. He couldn't sleep on the ground in this weather, and there was only one wagon. So she squared her shoulders and said thank you—she even gave him a smile. He really was a good man, a very good man.

అ

The rain poured, soaked, and drizzled down for two solid weeks. The Sharp family was ecstatic, at least for the first week. Their crops were in dire need, and Rebekah certainly could understand their joy in welcoming new hope for corn and peas and hay. She wondered if it were raining at Thornapple, imagined those fields greening even in the rain, the smell of Firefly's damp hide, the sound of rain on the roof at night.

Living with the Sharps was far different from life at Thornapple. Here were six children nine and under who quickly learned they could demand her attention every waking minute. Shy at first, they didn't take long finding out she was fun to climb on and would play guessing games, give them rides on her shoulders, and create fantastic paper dolls from any scrap they could wheedle away from Mama's safe keeping. Molly particularly loved those paper dolls and would crawl up in her lap clutching any size of paper she could collect. "Miss 'Ebekah, make dolls," she would say, and Rebekah always did, glad that somehow in her tomboy-ish childhood she had learned how to do this.

Amanda Sharp tried to persuade her guest to take her and Mr. Sharp's bedroom. But Rebekah wouldn't hear of it, so she shared a room with three little girls, including the little "knee baby" as Amanda called her toddler. The first time Rebekah woke up soaking wet and realized children on both sides of her had failed to make it to the slop jar, she thought maybe she was crazy for turning down the nice privacy of the Sharps' bedroom. But of course that was only for a short spell while she plundered around looking for dry clothes and bedding. Amanda apologized the next day and said with a grimace followed by a smile, "It's the rain does it. They hear the rain and thinks they've gotta tinkle, too."

With Idus Sharp's help, Aden found himself a corner in Ben Ruark's general store for practicing dentistry since the weather was rugged. He'd ride in every day on Jolly or Jake, repair or pull teeth all day for farm folk who thanked good fortune for letting them see a dentist when it was raining and they couldn't do much else. Amanda Sharp insisted Aden had to have supper with them every day. "Bad enough you two newlyweds being separated all the rest of the time. You need at least to clap eyes on each other every evenin'. Anyways, you can't keep a camp-fire in this horrible weather."

Amanda was a marvelous cook, and Aden Robards took full advantage of her warm hospitality. Every day he brought a ravenous appetite with him. He ate so hungrily that Rebekah was embarrassed. These people would think she never cooked for him. She knew she shouldn't care one way or the other, but somehow it did matter. It was particularly disturbing since she couldn't get close enough to Amanda to be wholly trusted in her kitchen. Amanda let her help in other ways, sweeping, dressing the little ones and reading to them, even washing dishes—but when it came to cooking, she wanted to do it herself.

But, for the most part, she and Amanda got along well. She gradually relaxed into a comfortable routine, becoming accustomed to Amanda's quiet ways and Idus Sharp's crudeness. Sometimes she almost forgot what a strange relationship she had with Aden since, after all, she was putting on such a good front for the Sharps. Or so she thought.

One day she and Amanda were hanging wet garments on backs of chairs drawn up close around the kitchen stove. Amanda had just finished telling Rebekah how she and Idus had met at her cousin's wedding. She hung one sock, then bent over searching in a pile for the sock's mate as if they had to be hung together. Her lips pursed out in a way Rebekah had already discovered meant Amanda was going to say something she wasn't sure she should. Finding the sock, she straightened up and started talking again, looking only at the sock, not at Rebekah. "Don't know what you two done argued about, but you'd best not let too much water run under your bridges 'fore you patch up."

Rebekah faced her hostess with her own mouth gaping. "We haven't argued! Everything's—fine. I don't—"

"No, it ain't fine. I know separation when I see it. Ain't once seen that young man lay a finger on yer cheek nor anywheres else."

"But that's—no sign—"

"Shore is. But you can fix it, mind. I know it ain't my business. But—well, I like you. Both of you. And sometimes a body's gotta say what needs to be said."

"Thanks. I appreciate your many kindnesses. But—oh, my goodness!" She clapped her hand over her mouth, not sorry that Grady's overeagerness in hide-and-seek had caused the whole arrangement of chairs and wet clothes to collapse at that very minute.

"Grady Sharp! Go stand in the corner this very minute! And if you don't, I'm gonna get you with this here wet towel and blister yer legs!"

&

Rebekah wondered when it would ever stop raining. She had felt awkward with the Sharps at first because they were strangers, but now she felt awkward because Amanda was so perceptive. She was actually glad one morning when Aden asked her to go into town with him. He knew of two clients who'd asked him to put fillings in their teeth, and he'd need her to help him by handing instruments and preparing the amalgam while he drilled teeth with his sometimes-cranky hand drill.

One client was a scared, sweet little woman who closed her eyes tightly as soon as Aden began examining her problem. It took both Aden and Rebekah to pry her out of the chair when he was done. She'd been so rigid for so long she couldn't unfold. The other one was a young man who came late in the afternoon from his logging job. Aden cheerfully instructed him to wash his face in a nearby basin before he'd even look at his mouth. "Don't want you developing an infection from local contamination," he explained, grinning at Rebekah, who made a face behind the man's back. She wished he had washed more than his face.

As Rebekah followed Aden's meticulous instructions, mixing amalgam and handing him instruments, she listened to his running one-sided conversation with this young fellow named Pete. Pete grunted sometimes or flopped a hand up and down in answer to Aden's monologue.

"Now, Pete, this may feel like a sawmill in your mouth. Steady there. You take down some big trees today? Must have been pine. You've got signs of pine tar on you. All right now, steady there, Pete—hold on. Your tooth's been hurting you pretty bad, you said, so you can stand some pain now to get rid of it later. Think of it as fixing your saw blade so it will slice through the wood more easily. You'll be chomping some fine venison soon with this molar." Pete slapped a hand on one thigh and grunted, then almost gagged. Aden had to let him come up for air a minute and instructed Rebekah to give him some water before he began again.

"I just had a talk with Jesus about this tooth," Aden said as he continued. Rebekah looked around to see how the man took that information and saw his eyes stretch wide. Aden laughed. "I'm always glad to have His help. He knows every tooth in your head, I figure, since the Bible says He knows every hair on your head. Oh, you didn't know that? And you know what's even better? He thinks about us! Come on now, Pete— I'll be through in a minute. Listen to what I'm telling you. It'll help get your mind off this tooth. Got that amalgam ready, Rebekah? That's a little too much. There. Yes, the Lord God Almighty thinks about us! Says so right there in Jeremiah. It says, 'For I know the thoughts that I think toward you, saith the Lord, thoughts of peace, and not of evil, to give you an expected end.' See, He's thinking thoughts of peace, not of evil, and He's given me a lot of hope that the expected end is going to be really good for you. Now bite down on this piece of paper. Oh, let me see if I can rasp that off for you a bit. Rough as sandpaper. Your tongue will go crazy on that. Now—about that eating. You're going to have to go easy on it for a day or two. Tell your wife to fix you some good soup."

After Pete wobbled out the door, one hand on his briary jaw, Rebekah began to clean up. "Do you always talk your patients to death like that?"

"He wasn't dead. He'll be out in the woods again tomorrow, fine as ever with no toothache."

"Humph!" She wiped the metal table clean. "Just doesn't seem fair somehow—you talking so much, asking questions your clients can't answer."

"Yes, but think of it as my special nerve-calming recipe," said Aden, putting instruments in a small pan of disinfectant. "Works every time."

She couldn't help smiling at the jaunty pleasure in his voice. The man sure loved what he did. She sobered immediately as she remembered what Amanda Sharp had said, how they appeared to have had an argument. She supposed they really seemed like strangers to each other because that's what they were. All that Bible talk he'd thrown at Pete proved to her again that she and he weren't a good match and never would be. He spoke a foreign language she didn't plan to learn.

But she did like assisting him all the same and was disappointed when, for the next few days, he left her to stay cozy and dry at the Sharps'. He'd come in at night soaking wet from his ride out from town. Amanda would insist he and Idus should sit by the kitchen fire and dry out, though they both complained that they were hot enough as it was and what did she want, some steamed clams for supper? Then she'd laugh and tell them they were so far from steamed clams there was no comparison. Clams, she declared, wouldn't talk the horns off a billy goat. Idus, though disgruntled, did what his wife instructed as if he were fully aware that in this situation she was the boss.

One night, though, Aden was very solemn. Idus Sharp started conversations that soon stalled out until he stopped trying. The children still pestered Aden to enter their fun. During the meal they chattered noisily, trading with each other cornbread for bits of salt pork as they tried to involve both Aden and Rebekah in their argument about whether or not ghosts were real. Aden only grinned a time or two, ruffled Tom's hair one time, responded to Mary Beth's direct questions and no more. "No, there are no ghosts," he declared finally. Seeing Rebekah's odd look, he shrugged his shoulders. "At least I don't think so."

"I think Doc's off in another world tonight," said Amanda, trying to tease the baby into taking one more bite of smashed peas. "You young 'uns leave him be tonight, you hear?"

"Sorry. I'm not very sociable, am I?" Aden looked around at all of them, then let his gaze linger on Rebekah's face. "I'm worried about a patient who's probably going to be in a lot of pain tonight. Think I'll ride back over to his place. I had to pull four teeth today, and he's—it was rough for him." He pushed his chair back.

Amanda shuddered. "Well, do go help the poor man. Dear me! Four at one time."

"And they were solidly seated, too," added Aden. "I had to get another fellow to hold onto my patient, give me some leverage. Those teeth did not want to come."

"Then why'd you take 'em?" asked Amanda curiously. "Why not leave 'em in the poor man's head?"

"They were giving him all kinds of pain. He couldn't enjoy eating and had wasted away to a beanpole. Teeth were turning into his cheeks and would cause more and more difficulty."

"Oh, I see. Well, in that case—but if it was me, I think I'd hold onto that pain rather than try a worse one."

"About now he's probably wishing he'd done that," said Aden. At the door he looked back at Rebekah. "I'm afraid infection may set in, and—the man's wife has a bunch of kids to see to, so—"

"I'll be fine here," said Rebekah. "Of course do what you need to do." Feeling Idus and Amanda Sharp staring at her, she smiled and said again, "I'll be fine."

"Sure is a fine dentist you have there," said Idus Sharp after Aden had left. "If I ever have to have teeth pulled," he added, making a long face, "I hope I'll have someone around who'll worry about me like that."

"He'll be ready to worry about you anytime, Mr. Sharp," said Rebekah, amused at the way he then clamped a big rough hand over his mouth. Later, after the dishes were done and the children in bed, she sat down to weave cloth scraps while Amanda knitted and her husband snored in his chair.

The next night Aden didn't come to supper but sent word by a passing neighbor that he'd be nursing his patient all night. He didn't come back for three days.

The sun came out finally, and after one full, sunny day, Amanda accepted Rebekah's help tackling the weeds in her garden.

"Ground's still too wet. We're liable to ruin everything, us tromping around in the mud. My mom always said working in wet ground'd turn it hard as brick. But ain't gonna be much use to have a crop if'n the weeds choke the termaters an' beans to death."

Rebekah agreed. Sometimes you had to choose the lesser of difficult consequences. She worked tirelessly, hardly aware of the scorching sun's rays. She worked up a blister and didn't notice until small Maggie exclaimed over it.

"All work causes pain," she explained to the little girl while she hand-pulled grass from among tender tomato plants.

"I don't like work. I like to play," said Maggie.

"I guess, to me, work is play," answered Rebekah.

"You really love gardening, don't you?" asked Amanda, straightening to squint at the sun.

"I really do."

"You miss your home."

"Yes."

"Maybe—you'll have a garden again someday," said Amanda.

"Yeah, and I'll come see you, Miss 'Ebekah!" said Maggie.

"Maybe." Rebekah was glad Amanda hadn't taken the opportunity of lecturing her about being happy with what she had. She had no intention of becoming happy with what she had because she didn't plan to keep it. But Amanda Sharp didn't have to know that.

"I guess you like work, too, don't you, Amanda?" Rebekah

still said the woman's name carefully, feeling disrespectful to call someone older than herself by her first name, though Amanda insisted.

"No," answered Amanda. "Not really. I just—love my family, that's all."

જ

When Aden finally came back, he was leading a new horse, a bay called Banner. "Because of the single white marking below his forelock," he explained, running his fingers over the "white flag" as he introduced Banner to the Sharp family, all gathered in front of their house.

Rebekah stayed on the tall front steps hugging herself and staring at the horse.

"Come meet Banner, Rebekah," called Aden. "He'll be yours as long as we can keep him. We'll have to sell him sooner or later, but—"

Rebekah unfolded her arms but held her hands tightly fisted at her sides.

"He's real sweet, Miss 'Ebekah," said Molly, laughing as the horse seemed interested in eating her thatch of blond hair.

Rebekah approached the horse slowly. "How'd you get him?" she asked, still making no move to touch Banner.

"He's payment. For the tooth pulling. I know, a lot bigger payment than I usually get, a lot better than a few potatoes. His master developed quite a fever, and I wouldn't leave him. Now he says he has no cash. But he wants me to take Banner, his extra horse. I told him if he got the money together I'd trade back. In the meantime—"

Rebekah saw hope in Aden's eyes that both scared her and pulled her, but she didn't know why. He looked so tired, too, and she truly didn't want to be mean. Anyway, the horse was undoubtedly a beauty so, in spite of herself, she finally ran a hand lightly down his shoulder. Banner rubbed his head against her, and Aden burst into laughter. "I knew you two would like each other!" he said.

But as Rebekah lay that night in Aden's wagon (she had no excuse any longer for needing shelter from the weather), she promised herself she would not love Banner. Aden had said he was hers until they sold him or until his patient found enough cash to pay him. So—no, she wouldn't allow herself to love Banner. Everything in her life now was temporary. Life would begin again only when she got home to Thornapple. She chased a thought of using Banner as a means to go home. It couldn't be too far for her to ride in a couple of days or at least three. But then she'd have nothing when she got there, so what good would it do her? Somehow she had to arrive back at Thornapple with land-buying money in her hand, even if enough for only a few acres.

six

When Aden and Rebekah pulled out heading north, the Sharp children were all solemn, some even crying as they lined up on their tall steps to see "Miss 'Ebekah and Doc" off. Tom, whether amused by his sisters' tears or not knowing anything better to do, laughed nervously behind his hands. Even little Grady sobbed into his mother's skirts.

"Hush up, Grady!" his father commanded.

"Aw, Idus, he's scared with all his sisters cryin' like they are," Amanda whispered to her husband. But Mr. Sharp grabbed Grady up and said he'd stop his sniveling or else.

The last Rebekah saw of them, Amanda was cuddling her lap baby while waving the woven square Rebekah had just given her. Maggie, Mary Beth, Molly, and Sarah, blond heads bright in morning sun, waved with frantic vigor, using free hands to swipe at their noses.

Tom, standing on the ground to one side of the steps with his legs crossed as if he needed to run to the outhouse, stopped snickering long enough to yell, "Are ye comin' back?"

Aden called back cheerfully, "You never can tell!"

Rebekah waved until they rounded the curve to turn onto the main road. Then she had to dig out her own handkerchief.

"It's hard making friends and then leaving them behind," said Aden gently.

"Then why do you do it? Why don't you stay in one place?" she asked, unable to hide the squeak in her voice.

He grinned at her and reached out to wipe away a tear she'd missed where it streaked down her tan cheek. Almost invisibly she pulled away, and he grimaced as he attached both hands to the reins.

"The Lord told me to start traveling, and until He tells me to quit, that's what I plan to do." He answered her question with an added twist of stubbornness in his tone.

She didn't bother to respond. There was no use. She really didn't care anyway. He could travel all he wanted to. When she was ready to go home, she'd go, when she'd found a way to get hold of some cash. She looked back at Banner following the wagon with a puzzled look, as if he didn't understand this new arrangement, freedom only as far as his tether allowed. She'd get down before long and ride him alongside the wagon or maybe not so close.

❧

Aden had visited Banner's former owner before leaving and had offered again to square away his bill in some other way, but the man was adamant that Aden should take Banner. He insisted Aden had saved his life, and giving him this horse was the least he could do. Whether or not he deserved it, Aden was glad to have the spare horse and happy to see Rebekah enjoying him. *I'm counting on you, Banner, old boy. Maybe you can win her over for me.*

In Perry, Aden found a lot of work. They set up camp on the edge of town one evening, and he rode into town on Jake the next day. It didn't take much to persuade the proprietor of the drugstore to allow him to set up there. Rebekah became more adept at holding tongues, mopping out cavities after Aden had mined around with his hand drill, and handing over the right instruments. She knew now when Aden started to pull a tooth that he'd want either the ominous heavy forceps or an extraction key, according to how difficult it was. If he were preparing to fill a tooth, she could often guess which excavation instrument he wanted or at least be able quickly to hand him the chisel he asked for. She also knew better how to talk to those waiting, how long certain jobs would take, what they could expect. She was always glad when it was possible for the waiting patients not to be in full sight of Dr. Robards's chair with its current occupant.

"Children will work themselves into a frenzy while watching," she said to Aden.

"And adults are even worse," said Aden, flashing her a smile.

"I guess we—adults—have seen and experienced enough that we know how to be really scared." She put her own hand to her mouth with a shudder.

Aden laughed. "Your teeth are in such good shape—you have no idea what my patients go through. You know, it would probably make it easier to be sympathetic and helpful if—"

"Oh, no, you don't! We've been through this before!" exclaimed Rebekah, sealing her lips shut; her brown eyes were alight with mischievous challenge.

Aden put his hands on his hips and stepped closer to her. She moved back a step. Suddenly he reached out in an incredibly quick step and clasped one very strong arm around her like a vise. "Let me see if there's not an old molar or wisdom tooth that needs to go," he said, his face twitching with controlled laughter as she squealed and squirmed.

She applied her elbows and was gratified to hear his grunts and a sharp "Ouch!" or two. But somehow in the process of thrashing for freedom, she landed more firmly in his grasp than ever, this time encircled in his other arm. He put a big hand up to cup her jaw as he supposedly prepared to examine her mouth. She screamed in agitation, twisted hard in his arms, then suddenly found herself face-to-face, nose-to-nose with this man she'd married. His eyes sparkled with laughter and mischief, and something else spellbinding in its intensity compelled her attention. She tried to turn her head, not to look, but she couldn't avoid his laughing blue eyes, which drew her farther and farther under his spell. She knew what he was going to do before he lowered his mouth to hers. She knew but could not do anything about it. He kissed her, and she couldn't resist. For an eternity packed tightly into one short minute, she was in another world where everything was all right and good. The trees tumbled upside down; the sky became a smooth, perfect lake; and, far away, birds' songs created a sweet concert.

Then Aden pulled back and looked down at her with such— was it triumph in his eyes? Anyway, a rush of fury shot through her. She had no more sense than a wild horse finally penned. Breaking away, she ran into a nearby wood and would not respond to Aden's call. She knew she was stubborn and unreasonable. After all, no matter what, she had married the man, and he had every right to kiss her. And she had even liked it! That was just it. She was far from willing to give up her own dreams of owning Thornapple to follow a dentist wherever he went. He knew that from the start, and he'd have to keep on knowing it. She would never let herself love that man!

Several times after that episode, she noticed warmth emanating from Aden's smile, even a certain electricity in his touch as their hands met in the exchange of instruments. But she would not look him in the eyes. She avoided his touch carefully. They could talk. That was safe as long as she was on her guard.

In camp sometimes they had long, comfortable talks when the day was done, the horses fed, and supper put away. As long as she had some space and didn't feel threatened, she was more and more willing to talk. She was glad she and Father had kept up with current events because now she could talk with Aden about Henry W. Grady's agricultural ideas for the emerging South and speculate as to what would become of Star Route Criminals, post office and stagecoach officials accused of stealing millions of government money.

She noticed how eagerly Aden perused the *Macon Telegraph* whenever he could get hold of it and was glad he left it lying for her to pick up and enjoy. Many conversations sprang from stories they'd both read. But one of their main subjects for discussion was Banner. Though Rebekah had been slow to accept him initially, now she often bragged on this big brown horse with the white blaze almost as enthusiastically as she ever had raved about Firefly.

❧

"How are your parents getting on at your aunt's?" Aden asked Rebekah one afternoon as she stowed a rare letter in her apron pocket.

She shrugged one shoulder, then peered around a curtain to see if any patients were showing up.

"Business is slow this afternoon," said Aden. "Might as well rest a few minutes while you can. Come, Rebekah—sit down. How is your mother?"

Remembering how understanding he'd been of Mother, Rebekah broke her own resolve not to talk about family and explained that she didn't think Aunt Constance was being very patient. "Father doesn't say much. He wouldn't want me to worry. But it's what he doesn't say that bothers me. He never mentions Aunt Constance getting up in the night with Mother or taking her for a walk or even helping her dress. He did say that Mother doesn't like Aunt Constance's parrot and that Aunt Constance has tied an elaborate knot on the door of its cage to keep Mother from letting the bird out."

Aden smiled. "I can get that picture."

A howl of fear and dismay brought Aden and Rebekah to their feet simultaneously. Two women dragging a young boy struggled into the room. The boy's mouth was bleeding profusely, so Rebekah grabbed clean rags immediately. Aden began crooning a silly song to pacify the child while he picked tooth after broken tooth out of his small mouth: "Possum up a hollow, rabbit in a tree, shaking down a dollar, for you and me."

Rebekah mopped blood as fast as she could. She thought she'd seen some pretty bad sights, but this one topped any yet. "What happened?" she asked as the child's howls subsided somewhat into gurgling sobs.

"Fell out of a tree," said the boy's mother, taking a quick swipe at her own sweaty forehead and managing in the process to smear blood on her face.

"He's the littlest one in a group of boys as was a-playin'," explained the other woman, "an' the big boys dared him to climb to the tippy top of a sapling oak. They egged him on till he went one limb too high and the tree spilled him, dumped him prob'ly fifteen feet. Wonder he didn't break more'n his teeth."

"He crashed into a limb or two on the way down, looks like," murmured Aden. "Appears to be baby teeth, though. You're going to be fine when it feels better," he assured the little boy with a big wink. "In the meantime, you're going to have to drink a lot, not eat. You like milk?"

"Oh, he can drink milk like cows was goin' dry tomorry," his mother assured them. "I done told them big boys to leave this one alone. He thinks he's big as they are, can do anything an' everything they do an' then some."

Aden had left the little boy and, putting a finger to his lips, slipped quietly over to the curtained doorway. With a sudden sweep, he pulled the curtain back as he said, "Next patient, please." A cluster of dirty little boys gasped and jumped backward, each one clamping a hand over his mouth. Aden laughed jubilantly. "I declare this little one the bravest of you all," he said.

During the ride back to camp that afternoon, Aden said to Rebekah, "You should see yourself. There's hardly a scrap of that gray dress that hasn't been spattered with blood."

"Thanks a whole lot," she said, making a face. "I've never seen so much blood at one time. How a small mouth like that could make that much blood, I don't know."

"You dealt with it very well," said Aden, flashing her one of his big smiles.

"Not that it was easy," she answered, steeling herself not to get all fluttery over his fantastic smile.

"I think blood is beautiful," said Aden. "It's the color of life, you know."

"I suppose," said Rebekah doubtfully.

"But it is. Without the red blood racing through our veins, we'd be laid out in the churchyard, you know. And without Jesus' blood shed for us on the cross, we'd have no hope for eternal salvation."

Rebekah bit her lip. "How can you be so sure? Of God's promises, I mean. How can you believe all that about eternal life when you can't see, feel, or smell God?"

"Oh, but I can." Aden laughed.

"Can what?" she asked, wondering how they'd gotten onto this subject again.

"Can smell, hear, and feel God. Remember the smell of lightning after a storm?" he asked. "Well, that was God's power. I saw it; I heard it; I smelled it and even felt it once when I was standing in water. Thought I'd end up in heaven right then, but when I opened my eyes, I was just standing in the rain right on. Yes, ma'am, I've felt God's power, feel it every day in some way or another."

Rebekah decided it was time for a good run and spurred Banner forward. Soon the two were racing their horses along the country road, and, as usual, it was obvious Banner was going to win. Rebekah forgot momentarily about the fence she'd erected around herself and laughed as merrily as a child when she rode into camp three full horse's lengths ahead of Aden.

The Fourth of July found Aden and Rebekah still camped on pancake-flat land near Perry. "Get ready to go to the celebration," said Aden that morning as he finished his cornmeal mush. Rebekah hurried to clean their bowls while Aden got the horses ready to go. It would be nice to see how these folks observed Independence Day. She remembered once long ago going to LaGrange for their celebration. They'd stayed at Aunt Constance's then and sat on her porch to watch a raggle-taggle parade go by.

Here in Perry, several men had dug out their confederate uniforms and paraded through town with a band that was funnier than it was good. Guns were fired at noon, but the highlight seemed to be sausages on a stick sold by a Mr. Gosnell. It was from him they learned the sobering news.

"You read the *Telegraph*?" asked Mr. Gosnell, passing Aden two sausages.

"No. What's the news?"

"Man shot the president two days ago."

"Shot President Garfield?" Rebekah's hand flew to her mouth. "Is he——?"

Mr. Gosnell shook his head. "He's not dead. But it's really bad."

"Have they any idea who did it?" asked Aden.

"Paper says he was some kind of Republican, but not the same as President Garfield. You'd think a Republican could just be a Republican and be done with it. Anyways, this man was mighty mad about not getting a government job he thought he should have. Shot Garfield, and him only president since March."

"That's a sick man would shoot a president, even if he is a Republican," said the next sausage customer at Aden's elbow.

Aden gave the fellow a stern look. "It's a sick man who would shoot *anyone,* especially a president, whether Republican, Democrat, or anything else."

The man shrugged his shoulder. "Don't have to get so stirred up," he said, his hands twitching in his pockets, his gaze following the vendor's hands as he worked his sausages.

Rebekah's thoughts whirled with the magnitude of the news they'd just heard. "Maybe the paper's wrong," she said, taking a cautious bite from the end of her sausage. "It seems so incredible that when we started out today we thought the president was safe and sound. Yet even right then he'd already been shot, and we didn't know anything about it. It seems so strange."

"A lot of things are strange. Some we can't help. Some we can," said Aden in a distant sort of way, as if he were talking about other things suddenly.

Rebekah looked up, then turned to follow his gaze. The man had drifted over to his family and apparently was explaining to his thin wife in her limp dishrag-colored skirt that the sausages cost too much. But what could Aden be thinking? Hadn't the man just now displayed a poor attitude concerning the president's assassination? Surely Aden wouldn't—but, yes, he would.

"Give me three more of those sausages, please, Mr. Gosnell," said Aden with brisk determination.

"Sure, Doc. Thank you, Sir." Mr. Gosnell's small eyes twinkled knowingly in his shiny, broad face.

Rebekah ambled toward a shade tree while Aden performed his mission. The sun was so hot, it felt as if she were roasting like her sausage. And the sausage now somehow wasn't as tasty as before. It became even less tasty as she saw Aden, after handing sausage sticks to all three children, push his own into the hands of their mother. The woman stared at the sausage in her hand, then up at her husband, still not taking a bite.

The man scratched his nose vigorously, then shoved his hands in his pockets and hung his head, which must have been some kind of approval since the woman took a quick bite, then held it up for him to sample also.

"Did he say thank you?" asked Rebekah when Aden returned to her side.

"No. Guess he didn't know how."

Before she could open her mouth to comment, a man in confederate grays with pins where all the buttons should be came hobbling up. "Ain't you the tooth drawer?" he asked, laying a hand gingerly against a swollen jaw.

"Something like that," agreed Aden with a grin.

"Well, Doc, I wondered—reckin you could take a look at this here tooth? It's a-jumpin' like a frog in a fryin' pan, an' I'm plum wore down with the pain."

Aden put a hand on the man's shoulder to stop him from setting his mouth agape right then and there. "Step a little farther from the sausage stand. We don't want to hurt Mr. Gosnell's business, do we?" He winked at Rebekah and whispered, "I'll be back."

That night around their campfire Rebekah asked, "Did that man pay you for looking at his tooth?"

"I didn't just look at it. I pulled it for him. He was in such misery; it was pitiful. And, no, he didn't pay me. He didn't have any money. But he listened to me while I told him about God." Aden chuckled. "That was good enough pay to me."

"How can you keep doing that? You should be paid for your services," she said, a tone of belligerence creeping into her voice.

"Rebekah, I'm not out here just to make money. If I were, I'd be beating on every door, I guess, for business. Or I'd be set up in a respectable office somewhere. But I'm out here to help, first and foremost."

"And when you've helped everybody and have nothing left yourself?" she asked too quickly.

"I'll always have what I need," he said steadily. Adding another stick to the fire and watching sparks fly upward, he said again quietly, "We'll always have whatever we need. And more."

He was so definite. There was no space for argument. Yet she felt argumentative. If she only had the money owed to this overgenerous dentist, she could buy several acres of Thornapple and a horse or two also, as well as that new guano she'd so looked forward to using. Squeezing her eyes shut, she listened to crickets making their up and down waves of sawing sounds, the same concert she would hear if she were at Thornapple. But there she'd hear Father's footsteps in the hallway instead of leaves rustling from an unknown forest creature. She'd hear water boiling in the teakettle instead of horses shifting their weight. She slung her braid over her shoulder and gazed again into the fire. There was no use dwelling on things lost right now. In due time she'd figure out a way to get Thornapple back.

"President Garfield has five daughters and two sons," she said as if that had been the subject of all her thoughts. "I didn't know that until today."

"I hope he pulls through," said Aden, standing up and stretching. "Hey, did you hear that? Someone's shooting a cannon. Or that's what it sounds like."

"It's still July Fourth," she said wistfully.

❧

One afternoon later in July, when they were camped outside Macon, Rebekah cut herself when she attempted to unscrew a rusty cap from a bottle of disinfectant and the bottle's neck broke in her hands. Aden chided her for not seeking his help, and she snapped back that it was better she cut her hand than for him to. Little help he'd be as a dentist with a bummed-up hand. To which he replied with a smug grin that he wouldn't have cut himself.

"Does it hurt much now?" he asked as he completed her bandage by tying a neat knot of cloth strips at her wrist.

She was so aware of his nearness, his warm breath against her hair as they both inspected her bandage. She grimaced as she raised her hand to relieve the throbbing and stepped back to put some distance between herself and Aden.

"No, not much. Did I spill all the disinfectant?"

"Doesn't matter. Don't worry about it," he said cheerfully. "I guess you know you've earned yourself a vacation."

"What do you mean?"

"You can't hold tongues, cleanse instruments, and mold amalgam with that big bandage hampering you. You'll have to stay in camp a few days. Or just sit and watch," he added, collecting shards of glass into the jagged bottle and turning a big smile her way.

"Oh. Well, I suppose I could use some time in camp to—" She hesitated. What exactly would she do? Riding Banner, washing clothes, and weaving cloth strips would all be difficult. But not impossible. And how good it would be to have the freedom, the camp to herself. Actually, that could be very good indeed.

"You'll figure out something," he said. "You might even read a book. The very best book of all time, past, present, or future, is at your fingertips in the wagon anytime, you know."

"I suppose you're talking about the Bible."

"None other. 'Thy word have I hid in my heart that I might not sin against God,' " he quoted with obvious cheer.

She leaned against the door facing of the lean-to room loaned them at Crane's General Store. Still nursing her hand, she cocked her head to one side, watching him put his instruments to soaking for the night.

Just then Mr. Crane appeared with a blackberry pie baked golden brown with purple juices congealing around the edges. "Thought you could use this," he said with such marvelous pride. "My Sarah says even dentists need sweets sometimes."

"Oh, this dentist takes sweets whenever he can," said Aden, leaning over eagerly to take an appreciative sniff of the pie.

❧

Rebekah was already disgusted with her own idleness by the second day of being banned from dentistry work. The freedom gave her too much time to think about her own hopeless position. And too much time to consider her proximity to Aden's cash box. If only she didn't know it was there! But she would not steal; whatever she did, she wouldn't do that. She found riding Banner pretty awkward with her hand so sore. She had read everything in sight except Aden's Bible, even several chapters of an awesome dental textbook. She'd walked the countryside and awkwardly picked a few grapes and even some peas a nearby farmer's wife offered her. Now she'd managed to build a fire for roasting four ears of corn and for cooking the little handful of peas she'd shelled with such discomfort. It wasn't time for Aden, and she didn't know what else to do. She stood looking into the wagon, eying her basket of cloth scraps then her bandaged hand.

As she gazed into the wagon's dark interior, she suddenly became aware again of the little upside-down table, its curved legs sticking up like odd pillars. Ever since she'd joined Aden, she'd been curious about that table.

Oh, he'd explained it was just something he'd bargained for one day, that it wasn't a family heirloom, at least not from his family. But why had he kept it all this time? Why would a bachelor living in cramped space hang onto something that belonged only in a fine parlor?

"So why did he keep you?" she wondered out loud to the little red-grained table. "But—since he did keep you—" she continued, heisting herself with sudden energy from what they called her "stepping stump" into the wagon. She plopped to her knees and began to remove a tidy cloth bag of ginned cotton and a box of books cradled in the table. "Since he saved you, why not use you? I'm sure you're quite tired of putting your feet up. Yessirree, you're going to be our banquet table for tonight."

Turning the table right side up and sliding it to the edge of the wagon, Rebekah climbed back down and wangled it to the ground. It wasn't easy, but she tugged and pulled until she had placed it under a big gum tree. She looked down at her hand and bit the side of her lip. "Jumping like a frog in a frypan," she said, mocking the little man in his own pain at the parade. "No matter, I'm going to serve a delicious, elegant dinner. And I know where some beautiful blue spiderwort is blooming. They'll be perfect in an empty medicine bottle."

She didn't stop to think too much about why she was making a banquet. She certainly didn't consider why it became so exciting to see what new details she could add. She dragged out a couple of her own dainty handkerchiefs to use for napkins. Mrs. Crane's pie would do extravagantly well for dessert, and she'd serve it in their tin coffee cups. They would have the roasted corn, those peas, and some beef jerky for meat. She thought briefly of the smokehouse at Thornapple as it used to be, hanging with rounded hams. "But beef jerky it is this time," she said with a sigh, adding some candles to the small table.

She had never felt any shyer than she did when she heard Jolly's hoofbeats and knew Aden would be riding up in just a minute. Impulsively, she stood in front of the table and spread her skirts out to hide it.

❧

Aden could hardly believe how much he'd missed Rebekah these two days. Could he dare to hope that she might have missed him, too? He certainly had noticed changes in her attitude lately. She'd talked to him much more, for one thing. And she hadn't seemed as cheerless. He'd been thrilled whenever she'd posed a question that allowed him to explain his faith in any detail at all. Now as Jolly's hooves pounded him closer and closer to "home," his anticipation of seeing Rebekah once more grew to a wonderful ache in his heart and soul. How had she spent her day? Would she give him one of those rare, shy smiles he so loved?

Better not be too eager. Rushing her was the worst thing he could do. He pulled on Jolly's reins instinctively as if slowing his horse would help him also to go slower in his relationship approaches to Rebekah. The memory of that kiss thumped in his heart, but he knew there wouldn't be another anytime soon.

He rode almost sedately into camp. And there she was! But

what was this? She was obviously hiding something. He forced himself to speak calmly as he slid off his horse, but he couldn't keep his gaze from swinging her way. She almost had stars in her eyes and was trying her very best to keep from smiling. About what? Could she be trying to surprise him?

When she moved aside and he saw the beautifully set table, his own very special little table, he let out a spontaneous whoop. It was all he could do to keep from picking her up and swinging her around in his joy, but he saw her shrink back involuntarily and knew that wouldn't do.

"How did you do all this?" he blurted out.

"With my one hand, thank you," she answered primly, almost as if she were trying to prove something to him.

"Well, if you can do this with one hand, I'd like to see what you can do when you have both of them again," he challenged. "Let me feed the horses right quick, and I'll join you. Something sure smells good!"

"Maybe it's the roasted corn," she said, letting her grin light up her face.

"You just wait, Lady, until I get back. Please let me rake those ears out of the coals," said Aden.

Aden rolled Rebekah's stepping-stump over to serve as his seat at dinner. Rebekah sat in their one chair. He not only raked the corn out of the coals but peeled the charred shucks away, too, exclaiming over each ear's plump beauty as if it were a gift he'd unwrapped.

"I guess the reason you're so delighted with the corn is that the imperfect rows of kernels keep you from missing those many, many teeth you can't gaze at again until tomorrow," said Rebekah, pulling a long face.

"Oh, no!" he said when he could at last stop laughing. "Rebekah, you are incredibly funny. Underneath all your bristle and reserve, you have a spicy sense of humor."

Rebekah's face only twitched slightly with a controlled smile as she sat with her hands in her lap. She bowed her head silently, waiting for him to say grace.

"Lord Jesus, Son of God," prayed Aden, speaking slowly in his deep voice that trembled a little with a hint of leftover laughter. "Thank You for this day, this time, this place, and for this delicious food and for—the hands that have prepared it." He paused in audible prayer as he sought in his heart to pray for his girl. He finished so quickly it was almost one long word. "In Jesus' name and for His sake, amen."

As the meal progressed, they were unusually quiet. It was as if they were visiting in someone's house and were afraid they might hold a fork incorrectly or commit some other faux pas. He didn't know what to say. He who, in Amanda Sharp's words, could "talk the horns off a billy goat" now could not think what topics to bring up. He felt he should hold his breath to keep everything as wonderful as it was these minutes. Yet if he was afraid to open his mouth, then perhaps it wasn't as wonderful as he hoped.

Suddenly she spoke.

"What on earth does it really mean when you say that— what was it?—at the end of your prayer. 'In Jesus' name and for His sake'?"

He lifted his eyebrows in pleased surprise. Dusk was coming on, and the candlelight flickered, making shadows on her face. She nibbled daintily at her corn, then laid it down and looked at him, ready for his answer. *Oh, Lord, here's another chance!*

"Jesus taught His disciples to pray that way—using His name. It's like—having a very excellent lawyer when you're in trouble, a lawyer who will defend you no matter how guilty you are and will guarantee you receive your requests no matter how poor you are."

A whippoorwill called from deep in the forest. Not far away another one answered. A moth flew into their pool of light and began circling one of the candles until Aden flipped it away. In the process, some hot wax splattered on his fingers.

Impulsively, she reached out with her good hand to help him. He smiled and assured her it was all right. She blushed and, hugging herself, looked off into the darkness for a minute. *Now she will forget what we are talking about,* he thought. But he was wrong.

"And the next phrase?" Rebekah asked, looking back at him. " 'For His sake'? You don't really mean that, do you? We ask for what we want, and it isn't for His sake at all. I suppose we say that to make ourselves feel less greedy somehow."

He finished his second ear of corn and picked up a strip of beef jerky to gnaw on. Staring at the candle flames a minute, he then dared look into her beautiful dark eyes. "When I pray, I'm always making mistakes. I can't keep my mind focused always on God and be able to pray as He'd want me to. But my desire is to please Him, to ask for things He's taught me to want—wisdom, patience, love for mankind, longsuffering for those who try to harm me. My underlying desire is to please God, and so I pray for His will to be done, or in honor of Him, 'for His sake,' meaning whatever isn't right for me I want Him to please strike off."

"And you'd really mean that, something you really wanted, even thought you needed, you'd say 'strike through it' just because it didn't please God?"

"Oh, yes. Yes, I would!" he declared. Then, seeing her troubled disbelief, he suddenly dropped the subject and said, "Do we get the pie now? I'm guessing we eat our pie before we get water to drink since we're using cups for dessert dishes."

She stifled a relieved giggle. "That's right. Mrs. Crane's blackberry pie. It reminds me of my mother's pies. She used to make the most wonderful pies—my goodness, Aden, what is the matter?"

Aden had suddenly jumped up from his stump so quickly he almost overturned a candle. Now he was feeling in all his pockets. "I've a letter for you. From your father. Here. Here it is. I'm so sorry I forgot it. You had everything looking so pretty—I forgot all about it until you mentioned your mother's pies."

"It's all right," she said, taking the wrinkled envelope. "I doubt a few minutes will make any difference in my reading Father's letter. He probably wrote it weeks ago. Come now and eat your pie. And tell me again why you're keeping this little table when you'd have so much more room in the wagon without it."

"But you see what an elegant thing it is. Surely you wouldn't want—"

"I didn't say anything about throwing it away, Aden. I just wondered. That's all."

"Is it in your way?" he asked suddenly as that possibility hit him.

"No, it doesn't matter to me," she said with a nervous laugh. "It's your table and your wagon. You can do whatever you please." There was no mistaking the thorny prickle rising in her voice.

He cleared his throat.

"Rebekah, of course it's your table, too, your wagon and your table." He leaned toward her, saw her look down at the envelope in her bandaged hand. When she looked up, it was with the firm, controlled gaze to which he'd become so accustomed, very removed from the laughing, almost teasing girl who'd set this tasteful table, who rode Banner so happily as if all were right and good. Would things ever really be right and good for them? *Oh, Lord, I have to hope!* She had set the table, and she had sparkled with the fun of it. But she had no idea that to him this table was symbolic of the home he wanted to establish—with her!

"I'll put things away while you read your letter," he said, standing up carefully so as not to send candles and flowers spinning.

"Oh, no, I'll read it later," she said quickly.

But he was already behind her, placing firm hands on her

shoulders, pushing her back down into her seat. "You will read your letter right now before it grows a minute older."

She turned her face up to give him a brief smile, then eagerly peeled open the envelope.

seven

July 1, 1881

Dear Rebekah,

I hope you are well and enjoying your travels. It does me good to think of you and Aden meeting so many interesting people and seeing the countryside. I'm sure it isn't that easy fixing all kinds of tooth problems and camping out in the heat and mosquitoes. But it's the way things are, and I hope you've gotten over your home-sickness for Thornapple.

I wish I had better news for you, but the truth is your mother is worse. Constance and I have to watch her at all times because she will suddenly walk out of the house. Twice I've had to go after her when she escaped and traveled as much as three miles. She always insists she's going home. No explanations do any good. She doesn't understand that this is home now and that Thornapple is no longer ours.

You will probably laugh about this. Mother managed finally to release Constance's parrot from its cage. The bird then flew out an open window and hasn't been seen since. Of course, Constance is beside herself. And I am really sorry (for Constance, not the bird!).

I did tell you, didn't I, that Mr. Jones bought Thornapple, or most of it anyway.

Joshua hasn't written since he left Athens. I thought he was going to Atlanta but have heard in a letter from Nancy West in Hogansville that a relative of hers saw Josh in Watkinsville a few miles south of Athens.

I can't help worrying about him. I'm actually glad your mother isn't aware enough to worry about either of her children.

I'm counting on you, Rebekah, to hold up this family's honor. Be good to Aden, and he will be good to you.

Warmest regards,
J. W. Thornton

Rebekah hardly noticed Aden stacking their plates, washing them at the spring, adding wood to the fire, feeding the corncobs to the horses, and talking gently to them. Through her father's letter, she became absorbed in thoughts of her parents, the smell of yeast bread baking in Thornapple's kitchen, the very feel of a brisk wind on Monarch Mountain, the soft stir of Talking Tree's pine needles. Mother was homesick, too. She'd gotten worse. She needed to be back at Thornapple. She needed her own daughter to nurse her. How dared she, Rebekah, begin to enjoy life here when her parents were being bossed around and scolded by Aunt Constance. Yet how could they ever go back to Thornapple? Mr. Jones had purchased it, and Mr. Jones wouldn't easily sell.

Numbly, she stood and picked up the soiled napkins to stash away for washing later. Taking a candle, she headed for her own private side of the campsite. When she returned, Aden had stowed the table away and was sitting cross-legged close to the fire, trying to read one of his many books.

"How about a chapter in *Pickwick Papers*?" He patted the chair next to him.

"I—I'm pretty tired. I think I'll crawl in the wagon."

"Rebekah—everyone's all right—aren't they?"

"Yes. Well—no, not really. They're not at home. Good night, Aden."

He jumped up. "Rebekah, if they're in trouble—"

"No. No, they're all right, I think. Thanks—for cleaning

up. My hand will be fine very soon, and I'll be able to do everything again."

He slammed one fist against his book, sighed heavily, then sat back down by the fire. She knew he was exasperated. But she wasn't sure why. Was it because her hand had caused inconvenience? Or was it because she wouldn't read her letter to him?

Later she lay in the wagon with eyes wide open trying to think of some way to buy back Thornapple, just the house and barns. Mr. Jones wouldn't give anything away, but for enough money he could be persuaded. If only she had money!

Aden's breathing was regular and heavy beneath the wagon. He was sound asleep. Father had urged her to be good to Aden. Hold up the family's honor. *What honor?* The thought of that box of money only feet away tantalized her. She shook her head vigorously in the dark. She would not steal from Aden. Yet—he did have plenty, more than he needed obviously, the way he kept spending money on other people and not requiring them to pay. Why not take some for herself? And if she left, he would hardly miss her. He could get almost anyone to do the things she did. He'd done them by himself before she came. Suddenly she saw again his face burst into that eager, surprised smile when he saw the table setting. What if Aden really did care for her? After all, he had insisted she stay home rather than work with her sore hand. But of course that was to protect his patients from her unsanitary hand. And how did she explain his many other kindnesses, such as tonight, quietly cleaning up camp while she read her letter?

Wearily, she turned her body and lay on her side, cradling her cheek in her good hand.

She could find all kinds of opportunities to take cash from Aden's box. He wouldn't know about it, and neither would anyone else. He certainly didn't assess his savings every day, and, by the time he missed it, there could be any number of suspects in little Georgia towns other than her.

But—regardless of upholding the honor of the family—she had her own honor to think about. And stealing was a repulsive idea. No! She would leave Aden eventually and go back to Hogansville. Somehow she would buy a portion of Thornapple and take her parents home. But she wouldn't take Aden's money.

≈

It was the third of August when Mrs. Leavenworth came in the Forsyth, Georgia, drugstore where Aden was now set up. She wore a black lace handkerchief as a mask over her nose and mouth, but gorgeous hazel eyes full of intelligence twinkled above. She had silvery white hair swept back from a high forehead. She was dressed in a tailored outfit of the most beautiful burgundy Rebekah had ever seen. But as soon as this lady began to talk, it was obvious what she'd come for.

"She wants new teeth," Rebekah told Aden.

Her teeth had separated from her gums, and another dentist who'd been there two years ago had taken them all out. But he'd refused to make teeth or try to find any connection for her getting them. So ever since, she'd been able only to drink or gum very soft foods like mashed potatoes and gruel. Now she wanted to be able to eat again. And smile again. She had some money that was hers alone, and this was how she wanted to spend it. She would surprise her husband.

"Why wouldn't the other dentist make teeth for her?" asked Rebekah after Mrs. Leavenworth was gone.

"He was probably just a tooth drawer and wasn't set up for making dentures," said Aden.

"Can you do that? Make her teeth? I seem to remember a story you've told about being scorned because you wouldn't make teeth."

"Well, I haven't done it before. But I really think we can. I've thought a lot about attempting to make dentures and have read everything I could find. And now here's this lady with no teeth. I feel sorry for her, and I want to try to help. I didn't think we could create a set of teeth from scratch, silver plate, ivory teeth, or even a cadaver's teeth—all that. But now—now we'd only have to make the impression and the final fitting." Aden had sat down in the chair and stretched his legs out. He grinned up at Rebekah with one eyebrow cocked.

"All right. What's different? Why only an impression?" Rebekah propped on a tall stool and pulled a cleaning cloth back and forth through her hands.

"They have this new vulcanite stuff, a hardening rubber that's really good for dentures. The Goodyear Dental Vulcanite Company had a tight hold on it until this year. Their patent's run out now so it's possible for a dentist to order a finished set of teeth, vulcanite, porcelain teeth, and all simply by submitting a client's impression. Of course we have to pay, but not the added patent holder's fee. We'll just have to find out who can order them for us. I've heard of a dentist in Macon I think can help us. We'll need wax and plaster of Paris for building a model." He sat forward rubbing his hands together.

"But—how can you make an impression of teeth that aren't even there?" Rebekah was mystified. "And wouldn't it be awfully expensive?"

"Well, we don't worry about what kind of teeth she had before. She gets brand new ones that will look wonderful. They make them out of porcelain. Pretty sturdy, I think."

Rebekah smiled, remembering Mrs. Leavenworth's main reason for getting new teeth. "I hope they're sturdy. Mrs. Leavenworth is getting hungry for an ear of corn."

He frowned. "She won't be able to eat an ear of corn. That's expecting too much. But she'll fare a lot better than mashed potatoes and mush. As to cost—we'll have to see. But she said she had some money. I hope it's enough."

Even though Rebekah had tried extra hard to be cool to Aden since the night of her silly "banquet," still she couldn't help warming inside when she heard him include her in the work. It was "we" this and "we" that. She knew she was unreasonable to like being included yet to refuse even to hold hands with her husband. But it was an unreasonable situation. It had been from the very start.

The next week Aden announced happily that he'd received an answer from the Macon dentist. "We consult with him initially about how to make the model and purchase supplies from him. After that we'll probably make exchanges by stagecoach. We'll make an impression of her gums, and with her help I'll draw a picture of what she wants the front ones to look like. It's important for her to have a pretty smile."

"What if—when you're all done—she doesn't like them?"

"We'll do a good job. She'll like them." He walked around the campfire, cracking his knuckles in anticipation. "Anyway, for now we have the consultation and supplies to see about. It's a pretty good trip to Macon from here. Better leave at first light."

"Tomorrow?"

"No need to wait around," he said, beginning to bank the fire.

Rebekah got up as soon as she heard Aden roll out from under the wagon the next morning. She felt tingly with excitement at the thought of a journey into Macon. While she was building the fire, Aden came along from upstream whistling one of his hymn tunes. He'd shaved and cut himself again on his chin. Not for the first time she was amazed at his shaving out in the "wilderness" with no hot water. She couldn't picture her father doing that.

"You should have slept until the sun came up," said Aden, obviously surprised to see her awake. "No need for you to be up so early just because I have to go."

"Oh. I thought—I mean, it's not really that early. It's brightening in the east." She would have died rather than let him realize how disappointed she was that he didn't mean her to go. She set some coffee to boiling and then walked into the woods, purposely not returning until she heard him shout good-bye as he left.

It was a beautiful day for riding, the air not as humid as sometimes, the sky blue with huge, puffy clouds. Maybe she'd just go somewhere herself. After putting some dried beans to cooking over the fire, she sprinted away on Banner. She wouldn't be gone too long, and the fire would probably go out before it could possibly scorch those beans. Town center was only a few minutes away, but it was far enough for her mind to begin hatching ideas. They had just come to Forsyth, north of Macon, a few days ago. Surely they'd be here for awhile. Was there possibly some job a respectable woman could do to make some money? She enjoyed thinking of her triumph as she announced to Dr. Robards her success in obtaining a position, perhaps something so good she would simply not be available to help him at all.

"Oh, don't be so peevish, Rebekah," she chided herself, shaking her shoulders in a symbolic attempt to rid herself of a bad attitude. "You know he was only too glad to let you have a day of freedom so you could do what you want to do. But of course he expects me to cook dinner and stay near camp, too. Well. Ha, ha! I'm going to see what else there is to do. I don't know what good all this dentistry practice is going to be to me in the future anyway."

She went to the post office, the millinery shop, the newspaper office, and two other stores. They all wanted to know if she wasn't the traveling dentist's wife. Then they jumped to the conclusion she wouldn't be around long. As Mrs. Griffin at Griffins' Dry Goods said, "If we did need somebody, we'd want someone who wasn't going to be leaving town the minute you learned how to measure yards and cut straight." The woman wasn't really unkind, but what she said stung.

Wishing she'd never stuck her neck out and asked for a job, hoping these people wouldn't say anything to Aden but ashamed to ask them not to, she chose needles and thread she needed, bought a fresh loaf of bread, and started out of town. The smell of the bread reminded her how much she missed having a real kitchen to work in. Oh, how she longed to be making a batch of bread about now, kneading it, rolling it, pounding it into shape.

Banner flicked one ear as they started by one of Forsyth's livery stables. "You probably know somebody, some horse in there, don't you, old boy?" asked Rebekah conversationally, glancing as she spoke toward the two-story building with rooms to let upstairs and stalls downstairs. Wondering idly how many horses might be in a livery stable this time of day, Rebekah suddenly thought she'd stop and see. What could it hurt? She never intended to ask for a job there, though as she tied Banner at the front she did think what fun it could be to tend to horses all day long.

The liveryman was as wrinkled as last season's haw apple with eyes of an astonishing pale blue. He didn't have much hair, but what he had was fiery red and hung down his neck, leaving the top of his head shining bare. Rebekah shuddered inside. Why on earth, then, did she hear herself asking this man if he ever needed an extra hand with his horses? Once the question was out, she didn't know how to take it back, but she forced herself to stand with her shoulders straight, her hands at her sides, while the little man considered her.

Mr. Baker, as he introduced himself, scratched his bald head and pursed his dry lips. Dropping his hand to hook his thumb over a wide leather belt, he brought his gaze to Rebekah's face, where it traveled down her dress to her scuffed shoes and all the way back up again slowly.

"I don't reckon we c'n use you around here. Don't really think as how you'd be suited to our kind—uhm."

Rebekah's face felt hot, but she refused to acknowledge what Mr. Baker was implying. "Wait," she said. "Before you say no, remember that looks can be very deceiving. Now maybe you need to look at my hands. See these calluses?"

Mr. Baker only glanced at her upturned hands. A grin had broken his mouth open, showing his lack of several teeth in front. "I weren't really considerin' yer ability, Ma'am. I was meaning I don't think you'd be comfortable in this here setting. Ain't you some kind of lady? I mean—if you're lost or something, maybe I could help."

"No. I mean, yes, I'm a lady. But—uh—"

"Then why don't you go along on home, you see, Miss, and—well, I'll probably never mention this to anyone. I ain't a mean sort, you know."

Rebekah's face stung now with embarrassment. Couldn't a woman ask for a job without all this harassment? "Sir," she said evenly, "your meaning is obvious, but I am quite capable of taking care of myself and have no intentions of being involved in anything that would bring dishonor either to myself or to your stable. It's just that I'm very good with horses—and I need a temporary job."

"Oh, I believe you, Ma'am, Miss—uhm. Who'd you say your father is?"

"I didn't. My father is counties away and not responsible for me."

"So—you're all alone then?"

Suddenly Rebekah felt a creepy tingle up her spine. This was not turning out well at all. This little man was getting the entirely wrong impression. "I'm Mrs. Robards. My husband is Dr. Robards, a dentist."

"And he travels, don't he? Yeah. My wife done been to see him, got a tooth pulled last week. So what you wantin' with a job at a livery stable? Makes no sense, if you ask me."

"I just—like horses. I'd like to be able to groom them. But of course my husband wouldn't approve of my working so I—uhm—"

"Of course. And you wouldn't be interested in working for free, I don't reckon."

"Well, no. Certainly not."

Mr. Baker scratched his neck, looked at Rebekah, then eased toward her horse. "You know, Mrs. Robards—I ain't interested in any more help around here than I've already got. But I'm not against doin' business with you. Now, for instance, if you was caring to sell this horse, I could possibly give you an offer. Possibly, mind you."

"The horse is not for sale," said Rebekah as she prepared to mount. "I'm very sorry to have bothered you."

"I could give you, say, seventy-five dollars maybe. It'd be stretching it a bit, but I s'pose I could do that," he mumbled, easing up to Banner as Rebekah put her foot back on the ground.

She cleared her throat. She didn't want him to know it, but she might be interested. She hadn't realized Banner was worth that much to anyone else.

"I did not come here with any idea of selling my horse, Mr. Baker. If you don't have any work for me, I'll be on my way."

"Mrs. Robards, I believe I could even go so far as to offer you one hundred dollars for this horse, only because I think I know somebody looking for one similar to him. And, of course, because I'd like to help you out."

Rebekah hesitated. This man was definitely not looking out for her; he was looking out for himself. If she knew the somebody interested in a horse like Banner, she could sell him for even more. But she didn't know who it was. Mr. Baker was ready to give her one hundred dollars, and that was a hefty sum. A twist of guilt prodded her to remember that Aden wouldn't approve of this sale. But he had said he'd sell Banner someday. And this was probably a far better price than he'd have expected.

"Would this person—suppose you tell me who it is so I can be sure they'd be kind to Banner. He's an excellent horse, and I'd really hate—"

"A gentleman wants a horse for his wife. She'd be gentle.

But ye'll have to trust me. I ain't givin' away no secrets."

In the end Rebekah walked away with one hundred twenty-five dollars tucked into her money pouch. She waited until she was halfway back to camp in a secluded spot to move her money pouch from her waistline to a safer place inside the front of her dress. In doing so, she took time to examine the money, assuring herself it was real. If only it were really hers! An idea, subconscious until now, caused her to catch her breath. She slid the bills back and forth in her hands, then slowly separated one wrinkled twenty from the rest, then a five, too. Tucking them in a fold of facing up under her collar, she looked around before walking quickly toward camp.

Aden would be very impressed (she hoped) with one hundred dollars and would not even think of the horse's bringing any more than that. After all, she had made this sale. She deserved to keep some for herself. It would make a very tidy beginning to her going-home nest egg.

≈

Aden picked over his bowl of beans, throwing out the worst ones, nibbling on a few, spitting out some that were unbearable. Rebekah had washed them several times in the stream and then cooked them some more since those not scorched still seemed rattly. Even after she'd picked over them until few were left, they were still terrible. She had never been so mortified as when she discovered she'd burned that pot of beans while she was gone to town. Yet Aden had not complained, said something comical like "new bean dish, huh? What's the name of it?"

At least the bread was good. It was especially good with butter Aden had purchased from a farm on the way back from Macon. "Almost melted," he said with a grin. "I took a little shortcut through a briary field; when I came out on the other side, I looked down and saw a yellow stream running down my leg, and I thought, oh, no, I've got yellow blood. But it turned out it was butter melting in my saddle pouch. Fortunately I was almost home and could set it to cooling in the edge of the stream. You must have ridden Banner to town to get this bread. I didn't notice him when I turned Jolly loose. Jake came running up, but not Banner. He out there beyond the thicket? You said you fed him and Jake. They eat all right?"

She cleared her throat. She hadn't thought it would be this hard. After all, wasn't it a good thing? So why did her throat feel as if it had shrunk to a tiny dry tube about to close up for good?

"Uh, I've got news." She fiddled with the end of her braid.

"Mrs. Leavenworth saw you in town, didn't she? She is so nervous, but I told her it would take me several days to get ready. She may be disappointed in the cost. But I'll remind her what a good set of dentures would cost in Boston, and then she'll be happy. This vulcanite's not cheap at all."

"How much?" she asked.

"In Boston they cost six hundred dollars," he said with a mischievous grin.

She gasped. "How much here, Aden?"

"I've got it negotiated down to around a hundred. I know. It's quite a sum. But I think Mrs. Leavenworth can do that. I'll go easy on her for my own work since it's my first time. I admit I'm a bit anxious about this, but it's so exciting, too, trying something I've never done before. So—she was ready to get started, was she?"

"Aden, I didn't see Mrs. Leavenworth. I–I—well, it's good news! I sold Banner today."

"You—*what?*"

Aden set down his bowl. She looked up and was stunned at how he had paled, his one-day's growth of whiskers looking especially dark.

"I sold Banner," she repeated. She pulled out the money and turned on a triumphant smile as she handed it to him. "You said you wanted to sell him sometime. Did you realize when you pulled those teeth you were getting one hundred dollars? Look at this, Aden! Isn't it wonderful!"

Aden took the money as if it might have a disease on it, held it awkwardly a moment, then began with meticulous care to straighten every crease and crimped corner. Rebekah was about to relax, thinking he really was pleased, when he spoke with the first harshness she'd ever heard him use.

"Rebekah, you had no right! It was my horse, and you had no right. To whom did you sell him?"

"You said he was my horse as long as—"

"As long as—but you weren't to decide when he should be sold. You had no right!" Standing now, he flexed his jaw as he looked down at the bills in his hand.

"Aden, I—" What could she say? She'd never dreamed he would be so angry. And she'd never dreamed his anger would bother her so much. She wished desperately for his usual quirky grin, but his mouth remained set in a straight line. "Aden, I—" she tried again, taking a step toward him.

He held up one hand as if guarding himself. "It's too late now, Rebekah. Don't even try to make it right. There's no right to it!" He gave her a hard glare, then suddenly stuffed the money in his pocket and walked away.

"If he was my horse, then why couldn't I decide when he should be sold?" she fired after him, but he kept walking.

She watched him go, her heart pounding with a strange fear—of what she didn't know. She put knuckles to her mouth to push back a sob. She would not cry. No! She would not cry. Because Banner was hers and she sold him, and she had nothing to cry about except missing her horse. There! How dare Aden treat her like a mere child and tell her she had no right to sell a horse he'd given to her. The more she thought about it, the hotter her blood sang in her ears and the less she worried about the twenty-five dollars still tucked inside her dress. It served him right to get only a hundred. He wouldn't have gotten any of it if it hadn't been for her. And she was glad she hadn't told him where she sold Banner.

For the next several days, Aden and Rebekah hardly spoke to each other. When they did, it was only about work, how much amalgam for a cavity, hold the tongue farther to the left, give the patient some water, and other such instructions from Aden; or, from Rebekah, questions about how much to charge or how long until he'd be ready for the little girl needing extractions whose sobs of dread had upset everyone.

For quite some time Rebekah had been the one to receive payments and give change. After she sold Banner and everything was in a strain, Rebekah began to be presented with temptations that at first shocked her. She'd been repulsed by her brother Josh's gambling and literally stealing the farm from her father. And wouldn't she be in the same category if she were to take a portion of Aden's money for herself? But the more she considered how he'd accused her of selling his horse, the more she thought about how she, too, worked every day, the more reasonable it seemed to do something about it. She held slimy tongues that slobbered and turned dry in her grasp; she emptied a bloody spit bowl and cleaned instruments—all for no pay. Why should it be only Aden's pay? She hadn't found a job at the livery stable or anywhere else. But she had one here. What she needed to do, it became clear to her, was to pay herself. Judging by his reaction to her sale of Banner, Aden wouldn't understand. So she didn't mention it to him. She quite methodically took a small, reasonable portion of each payment and squirreled it away. Aden paid her little attention, and it became more and more natural for her to divide the funds.

❧

Aden sat one August dawn near the campfire writing to his mother.

> *Dear little Mother,*
> *If only you were here, I would lay my head on your*

sweet shoulder and pour out my misery to you.

I have gotten nowhere winning Rebekah's affection. In fact, we are farther apart than ever. It's largely my fault, but I can't seem to repair the damage I've done. Mother, she sold the horse I had given to her. Granted, I did say we'd have to sell him sometime. But I'd decided I would never sell Banner because I saw she cared for him. When she sold him herself completely on her own, it stung me so deeply. I said things I very much regret. Why can't I call them back? My Father has forgiven me, but I haven't forgiven myself and haven't worked up enough courage or found the right situation to ask Rebekah's forgiveness.

She is so capable and self-sufficient she scares me. I'm afraid one morning I'll wake up and she'll be gone. Mother, do you think I was all wrong to marry this girl of my dreams? You would have told me I hadn't had time to know she was the girl of my dreams if you'd been with me. I leaped at a prize and now am recognizing it must not have been the prize God meant for me.

But I can hear you asking as you brush hair away from my brow whether or not I still love Rebekah. And, oh, yes, Mother, I do! I do! She has pushed me away so many times, I no longer try to touch her, but I long to. And this rift between us only shows me how much I've come to depend on her as a friend and companion. Mother, we were having such good times riding horses, talking for hours, chatting as we worked. I miss her now even though she's right here!

On another subject—Mrs. Leavenworth is happy with her teeth and has told her friends of our success, so I have two more denture customers now. One gentleman has been coming every Thursday to get more teeth out; I didn't want to take too many at one time. I've been talking to him about the Lord, and he's starting to go to church. He told me last Thursday that he and his wife have begun to pray together!

I received your letter dated July 20 when I rode into Macon to purchase materials for Mrs. Leavenworth's denture. I'm so glad it's a good year for apples. It's really good you've found a young couple to live with you and help you and Mr. Arrington. When you fold this letter away, please go out and walk down to my favorite appling place and absorb all the sights and sounds for me. I know you'll pray for me, and that's a great comfort. And please pray for Rebekah, too, that even if she never loves me, she can learn to love Jesus.

Please don't worry about me. If I actually mail this letter to you, I may be so sorry I brought you grief. But if I don't, I'll worry that I didn't keep my promise to let you know how I am doing.

I wish I could say Rebekah sends her love. But we'll have to wait on that. I know she would love you if she knew you! And I know part of the sorrow inside her is over being separated from her own parents.

Lest I end on an unhappy note—there's a brown thrasher pair nesting in a sweet shrub (a bush that has funny little sweet blossoms almost the color of a thrasher) at the edge of our camp. They are very loyal and defensive birds, and we dare not get too close to that nest or they'll fly right into our faces. The brown thrasher is a beautiful bird with the color of cinnamon on its back, a white breast well sprinkled with cinnamon freckles, and a long perky tail.

> Yours ever,
> Isaac Aden Robards

Aden had to write close to the edges of his few sheets of paper to get his last comments on. Then he thoughtfully reread the letter. He hung his head. It wasn't right to send such a gloomy letter to Mother. He scooted closer to the fire and held the pages out toward the flame, then finally folded them, making precise, neat creases, and stuffed the missive into his shirt pocket. He'd have to purchase an envelope and stamp in town. He stirred the fire and rose to get water for making coffee. Somehow he felt better, more cheerful, and even began to whistle as he ambled toward the creek.

৯

Rebekah, still in the wagon, heard Aden's whistling and felt a degree of tenseness ease away from her neck. If he was whistling again, maybe he at least was feeling better. She had to admit she'd missed his whistling. She began to brush her hair, preparing to braid it. It was going to be a warm day. She'd wear the blue cotton dress Mother had made for her before she got sick. It had a full skirt, buttons from throat to waist, with narrow ruffles around the neck and short sleeves. Libby Stokes was coming today to have some crowding teeth pulled. She was thirteen and had been so friendly when she and her father came to see Dr. Robards the other day. Rebekah had assured her the pain wouldn't be too awful and she'd be so proud of her pretty smile later. Libby had liked that blue dress, so she thought she'd wear it again just for her. *Maybe it will even cheer me a little.* She couldn't understand how very depressed she'd been for these weeks since she sold Banner. It was as if something very important died that day. But what? She hadn't had anything, so how could it die? Well, of course she missed Banner.

She'd worried for awhile that she might run into that funny little wrinkled liveryman someday, but it hadn't happened. As much as she would like to have dropped by to see if Banner were still there, she didn't dare renew acquaintance with that man. She didn't want Aden to talk to him ever. As angry as Aden had been over what he had learned, how much more irate he would be if he knew the whole truth! Well, she was glad her hand had healed quickly and she was able to work as hard as ever. No one could say she didn't keep everything in their dental corner swept and scrubbed to a high shine.

That was the day they began to talk again, but with a cool reserve, Rebekah thought. She missed the old Aden. But this was safer, much safer, so she wouldn't complain even to herself. And she'd gotten used to Forsyth, actually enjoyed seeing familiar faces on the street. Her homesickness had worn off a lot because now, she told herself, she was making progress toward going home. Maybe by the time they left Forsyth, she'd have enough cash saved up. She hadn't figured out how she was going to tell Aden she was leaving, what she was going to tell him, or even whether she was going to tell him. For now it was good just to work.

&

Aden had been fortunate in getting a fit for Mrs. Leavenworth's denture. She had come back several times but had been vastly pleased in the end. And her praise had brought other clients to Aden. Inevitably, however, with his limited knowledge, he fitted a client, an attorney highly respected in Forsyth, with less than satisfactory results. The denture pinched at first. Aden tried to expand it, but then the whole thing became loose. Finally, one day Mr. Osgood came to see him to tell him in a white-hot rage of how at a luncheon his teeth had fallen out into his plate or, worse still, had actually splashed into his bowl of potato soup. He told Aden he intended to make it uncomfortable for him to practice there any longer. Aden didn't give up easily, but when fewer and fewer clients sought him, he had to accept facts. Several friendly clients, who not only had received valuable help for their teeth but also were very thankful for Aden's Christian witness, brought Aden and Rebekah parting gifts, a dress length of perfect white lawn cloth for Rebekah, a salted ham, and various smaller gifts of preserves, bags of cloth scraps, and a notebook for Aden.

"I noticed you writing on backs of store bills and used envelopes, Doc, and thought you could use this," said white-haired Mr. Craig as he handed him the notebook.

Isaac Aden flushed right to his hairline both with pleasure and a bit of embarrassment that his writing habits had been noticed. But he was thankful for the paper and put it to work that very night, logging in descriptions of clients for whom he'd continue to pray. The farther he and Rebekah traveled north, the more names appeared in his book, and the more poems about the changing scenery—and about Rebekah herself.

eight

"We'll have to give our horses more rest now," said Aden, sagging against an oak tree at the top of a steep rise. "These north Georgia hills take the sap out of man and beast. But aren't they beautiful!" He waved his hand toward the scene before them.

The hill they'd just topped dropped sharply again on the other side. The red clay road ambled like a bright irregular scar down and up again, disappearing into dark green piney hills. Piney hills lapped into dark shadowed hills, and beyond them layers upon layers of misty, blue mountains drew one's gaze till they dissolved into a sky of brightest blue, active with puffy white cloud-ships.

Rebekah was in such awe of this, to her, new beauty that she said little. She was out of breath anyway from the steep climbs and equally as challenging descents. Their wagon twisted and turned along rutted clay roads and rocky ones. She was glad Aden often agreed to let her walk for a distance. But walking here was very different from the plains around Perry, and she was thankful when he stopped the wagon and waited on her.

Around three that afternoon, they approached a bountiful apple orchard. From one hill they looked down on lower slopes lush with row upon row of laden apple trees. There was a stream below, Aden said, judging by thick hardwoods following a valley floor. Awhile later, the road led them right through an orchard. Trees met in a canopy over their heads. Aden stopped the wagon and turned in his seat as she walked up. "These trees are almost as pretty as ours in New York!" he said, standing in the wagon to pluck one red-streaked apple, which brought a shower of raindrops onto his shoulders. He sprang down from the wagon and climbed a mossy bank to lean against a thick nubby trunk, pulling out his knife and peeling the apple. He held up a piece for her. "Sour, but crisp and good," he called. "Come on up." His mischievous grin challenged her.

Using one hand to hold her skirt from under her feet and the other to cling to a protruding root and then a small sumac bush, she reached him and accepted a slice of apple. It was good, juicy and so sour it made her whole face pucker, which brought a rare burst of laughter from Aden. He had laughed so little since she'd sold Banner.

"Well," he said, wiping his knife blade across his pants leg and folding it up, "we'd best be moving on. Cornelia's not far, I think. We can make it by night."

"What's in Cornelia?"

"Nothing much. But there'll be a place to set up, I think. There are a lot of people tucked around in these hills who need some teeth pulled."

She smiled at his cheerful optimism. "You're not wishing toothaches on anyone, are you?"

"No. Just know they have them, and I'm ready to help. Come—let me help you down," he said.

"Oh, no. I can do it fine. I think I'll just stand up here while you get started. That way the wheels won't splatter mud on me."

He looked at her oddly, then shrugged his shoulders. "I thought sure you'd be ready to ride by now."

"Not quite. I'm going to walk a little more, down this lane of trees. I'll ride again soon," she answered.

He started to say something but apparently thought better of it, leaped down the bank, climbed up on the seat, and clucked his tongue to the horses.

After Aden had driven on, Rebekah clambered down. In spite of sticky clay clinging to her shoes and making her already tired feet heavy, she relished this time to walk alone and dream a little. Looking ahead, she imagined all these trees at Thornapple instead of here. Why couldn't they grow apple trees there? Thinking of Thornapple, she immediately wondered if things were any better for Mother. She hadn't heard an answer to her last letter. She hoped Aunt Constance would have forgiven Mother by now for letting her parrot fly away! And what about Josh? She'd been pretty awful not to worry any more than she had about her only brother, even if he had done them so badly. She'd thought about him when she and Aden skirted Athens, but she had no idea where Watkinsville was, the place where Josh had last been seen. And she didn't think it wise to ask for any favors from Isaac Aden Robards. She'd have to see about Josh later. When she got home to Thornapple. Yes, when she'd revived Thornapple, at least found a bed and a chair for Mother, maybe even planted an apple orchard like this—well, then she'd send for her parents and even Josh. *Might as well dream big, Rebekah.*

"I reckin you probably don't mind too much, but if you keep a-walkin' the way you're a-goin', you'll step on a big black snake."

Rebekah stopped so quickly she almost sat down in the mud. A giggle erupted from the top of the bank. She first looked down to see that a large black snake was actually crossing the road in a leisurely manner. Then she surveyed the road bank to see who'd warned her.

There stood a young girl grinning down at her. She wore floppy overalls that hung around her small bones like rags on a scarecrow. Long, untamed brown hair fell over her shoulders, making her face appear small and vulnerable, but her eyes were bright and full of intelligence. She scrambled down the bank and stood barefoot near Rebekah, watching the snake continue its zigzagging, sometimes undulating, trek across wet red clay ruts and up the mossy bank.

"He just missed getting run over by a wagon," observed Rebekah.

"Oh, he'd a wriggled outa the way most likely. Where you goin' to?"

"Cornelia. Is this your father's apple orchard?"

"It's Butterfly Meadows," said the girl, smiling. "Belongs to my pa. You know my pa?"

"No. What's his name?"

"David Mayfield. I'm Cerise. It's a color Mama likes. I'm the youngest, and after seven others she'd run out of names, sort of anyway, and thought she'd use a color. Pa owns all this whole wonderful orchard. We live over the other side of that hill," she said, pointing through the trees. "You travelin' far?"

"Yes," Rebekah said, unable to keep from laughing at this chatty child. "We've come from Homer today. My—husband is—"

"That's him drivin' off leavin' you?" The child, seeing Rebekah's nod, put up a double fist to her mouth, and a sound like a train whistle spouted out.

Rebekah almost choked on a giggle. "Well, yes, he's letting me walk. I get so tired riding on that hard seat."

"Oh." Cerise let her hands drop to her sides and shifted her feet as if embarrassed. "Just tryin' to help," she explained. "Anyway, what's your name?" She sidled into a circle of sunshine, and Rebekah realized her hair wasn't really brown, but red, and that she had a thick sprinkle of freckles across the tops of her cheeks.

"I'm Rebekah. Rebekah Robards."

"Pleased to meet you. My ma always invites travelers to our house to eat and sleep. We'd be pleased if you'd come."

"How nice of you! But really we—oh, my, is that your father walking this way with Dr. Robards? I think I may be stuck in this mud. I haven't moved since you told me about that snake."

"Yes, that's Pa. Here—I'll break you loose." Cerise took time to be sure Rebekah could get up the bank before she took off through the trees, stumbling in her clumsy overalls.

David Mayfield was wearing a large hat that shadowed his rugged face. He walked with a decided limp but didn't let it stop him from catching up Cerise in a big hug. He smiled at Rebekah over the top of Cerise's bright head. "My daughter been talking your ears off, I guess," he said with a laugh.

"Mr. Mayfield, this is my wife, Rebekah," said Aden.

"And, Dr. Robards, this is Cerise," said Mr. Mayfield, letting the girl slide to the ground, then draping a hairy brown arm around her shoulders.

"What kind of doctor are you? You cut people open?" asked Cerise.

"I'm a dentist," he said with his large smile.

"Oh, good, our town hasn't had one in a year or two," said Mr. Mayfield. "Come. Ma's got a spread o' supper, an' she'll be so happy for some company."

"Are you sure?" asked Aden doubtfully.

The Mayfields, father and daughter, insisted heartily, would accept no argument, said surely the couple could at least stay until morning.

"You're only three miles from Cornelia now," said Mr. Mayfield, pulling out a dingy handkerchief to mop sweat out of his eyes. "If you decide to stay on here awhile, I can get you a spot in my brother-in-law's store where you can fix teeth. Maybe you could even do something about ours." He grinned and tapped darkened incisors. Cerise suddenly became shy and hid behind her father as if she might be a candidate for the dentist's chair. "Oh, you needn't hide, Babykins. We done pulled your teeth with a string tied to the doorknob!" He laughed as he clapped his big hat back on his head and hauled the little girl back into the open. "Ain't she a beauty now? You two ain't got young'uns yet?"

"Well. No. We've only been married since April," explained Aden as easily as if everything were perfectly normal.

"Oh. Sorry for bein' nosy. Wife says I'm always rushin' things. Just love to see people happy, that's all. Well, we're wastin' time here. You folks go on around to the house. We two'll meet you there. Turn at the next crossing an' look fer the two-story house behind a big oak tree. We'll draw you up some good, cool well water minute you get there."

It was as he described it, a two-story house behind a big oak tree. Only he'd failed to mention that not only did he have eight children but also a yapping tumble of dogs. Neither had he mentioned that the well was under the house, so he drew water for them right on the front porch by which time the dogs were settled down to only licking instead of barking.

"Yeah, this front porch well's the best thing I ever did, more'n likely. Saves my Betsy near 'bout two hundred steps a day, I reckin, havin' it here 'stead of out in the yard. Saves me some good number, too, when she hollers out just as I've pulled off my boots, 'Dave, I'm gonna burn your dinner if you don't bring me water this instant!' "

"Oh, he does love to exaggerate." A woman clad in a blue calico print dress joined them, her smile lighting her round face. She dried her hands on a large flour sack apron and tucked a wisp of moist hair behind her ear, the rest of her brown hair being caught up in a scrambled bun.

"Betsy, this is the Robardses. Aden and Rebekah. Hope I got that right?" For the first time the talkative uninhibited farmer seemed struck with shyness as if he weren't sure he'd used his best manners.

The screen door squeaked open and banged to one at a time for the seven other Mayfield children from Lawrence, a tall boy, almost man, down to Freddie, the youngest boy barely older than Cerise, who obviously felt it his responsibility to be her tormentor, pull her hair, tickle her neck with a straw, and pretend to pull a spider out of her ear. Between Lawrence and Freddie were five giggling, blushing, constantly jabbering girls, some of them quite ready for womanhood, it appeared to Rebekah. Each child was introduced, some ducking heads in a quick, shy nod, others bursting into their own volley of welcoming phrases.

Betsy and her girls set out a huge supper of boiled potatoes, green beans seasoned with ham hocks, cornbread, and pickles so crisp and sweet Rebekah could have eaten them all day. They had fresh-churned butter to drizzle over everything and tall, cool glasses of buttermilk. And after all that, the oldest daughter, Rosemary, brought out a huge cobbler in an enamel pan. She announced proudly that this was the first green apple cobbler of the season.

"So—do you think you'll stay around then?" asked David Mayfield after they'd all eaten sumptuously. He leaned back in his chair, ignoring a corrective frown from Betsy.

"You make it very attractive to stay." Aden looked at Rebekah and back at his host. "Could we let you know tomorrow? We'd better go along now and get our camp set up."

"Sure you can. Let us know anytime just so's the answer is yes." David eased his chair to a normal position and pushed himself up from the table. "I'll show you the spot I was talking about for your camp."

"Can we go, Pa? Can we?"

It sounded as if the whole family were going to escort them to camp, but Betsy put her foot down and insisted all three older girls stay and help clean up.

"You take some cornbread and buttermilk with you in case you get hungry before you come back to breakfast," said Betsy, her brown eyes sparkling as she handed Rebekah a jar and a cloth-covered basket. "And maybe—while Dr. Robards is busy on teeth, you could come talk to me—us, sometimes, hmm?"

"Oh, I am his assistant, you know. So I'll be working most of the time. But thanks! Thanks for everything. You are so kind."

"Please stay. I mean, camp with us and come here all you will. I feel—" Betsy held out her now-empty hands toward Rebekah, though Rebekah's were now occupied with milk and cornbread. "I'm sure we're to be friends, special friends."

The girls were giggling and chattering in the kitchen over the clink and bang of dishes and pans. The dogs were barking again as Aden jumped up to the wagon seat. Rebekah, amidst all the noisy activity, felt a steady quietness in Betsy that drew her like—like the solace of her dear old pine tree. Kind of a funny comparison. She smiled at Betsy.

"I'd like that," she said simply and knew it was the absolute truth.

A portion of Mayfield property lay outside the pasture fence. A creek flowed merrily nearby, and a thicket of oak and gum hummed with an evening insect chorus. This was where David Mayfield directed them. Cerise fetched water for Rebekah and would have stayed on to help, but her pa declared she'd be a nuisance and she must go home with the rest. Rebekah was relieved. As much as she liked the child, something about her made her very uncomfortable. She wasn't sure what. Maybe it was a feeling that Cerise was able to see right into the blackness of her heart.

Rebekah and Isaac Aden knew what each would do in setting up camp, and they began chores without speaking to each other after all the Mayfields had left. Rebekah had of late taken to unfastening the horses and grooming them, and she did that now. Aden shouldered his ax and went to chop down a dead oak David Mayfield had told him he could use for firewood. Betsy's offer of breakfast was nice, but they needed to make it on their own. He laid a fire ready for lighting the next morning and then busied himself leveling the wagon. He paused several times to glance over at Rebekah, taking a deep breath each time as if he were steeling himself for something.

The horses having already been fed this time at the May-fields', Rebekah had nothing else to do before preparing for bed, but she wasn't ready to climb in the wagon and sleep. It was still light, so she explored along the creek. Small frogs jumped in the water ahead of her footsteps making *ker-chunky* splashes. She didn't realize when Aden's ax blows stopped as she was absorbed in thinking how odd that Mrs. Mayfield, Betsy as she'd asked to be called, seemed like someone she'd already known.

"You really should be more careful, you know. Snakes are in abundance along a creek bank." Aden had come up beside her without her noticing. She flinched almost as if he had hit her and, in moving away from him, caught her foot in a root, almost tumbling into the water. He caught her by the arm and steadied her. "Didn't mean to startle you. But really you shouldn't—"

"I know all about snakes. They don't bother me in the least," she said, lifting her skirts slightly to walk on.

"Rebekah, I—need to talk to you."

Whatever he wanted to say could not be good; she could tell by the tone of his voice. It was not just a discussion about whether or not they should stay here to camp. Why had he deferred that decision anyway? He made it appear they would decide together, but that was ridiculous. It was his wagon, his business; he'd do what he wanted to do. But now he wanted to talk to her. Could he have discovered she'd been stealing his cash?

She stopped and turned toward him.

"Rebekah, I know—"

"No, you don't really know!" she blurted out, hugging herself against a sudden cool breeze. "There's no way in a hundred years you could possibly understand. I—I'm sorry, Aden." She looked at the tops of those two oak trees and beyond that a tall pine tree. She'd watch the bats wheeling. She wouldn't look at Aden.

"I'm trying to tell *you* I'm sorry, Rebekah. The horse—Banner—I thought you'd really started liking him—a lot—and that you—well, I was pretty disappointed when you sold him. But you were right. I had given him to you. I shouldn't have been so angry with you. Could we—be friends again?"

She turned her head cautiously and looked at him. Even though shadowed, his blue eyes dark in the dusky light, she could tell he was serious. His hands were at his waist, each thumb hooked over his belt in a characteristic stance. She studied his face for so long that he finally dropped his own gaze to his boots, then leaned over to pick up a spindly stick.

"You don't have to make it so hard," he said softly. "All I want is a little forgiveness."

"Well. Of course. Think no more of it." She hated herself for being so cold. But she couldn't afford to be anything else. She, after all, was the only one needing forgiveness. But she wasn't going to bring it up if he didn't recognize her crime. She had to remember it was for Thornapple and for Father and Mother. She had to do this!

He sighed heavily, lifted his hands in a helpless gesture, and turned back toward the wagon.

Hours later she turned very carefully, hoping the wagon wouldn't creak and give away the fact that she couldn't sleep. She had heard nothing from him since he rolled out his bedding under the wagon and called softly, "Good night!" She'd answered him with a cheerful enough "Good night" of her own. It was so difficult to be rude to someone who was so kind! She pictured him as he stood facing her out there by the creek. He looked so—so hopeful. There was something so very vulnerable about him, big man that he was. Could he actually, truly care for her? Tumbling right behind that thought was another disturbing one. What would it be like to love and be loved by a good man like Isaac Aden Robards? The happiness she saw in the Mayfield house, in the eyes of Betsy Mayfield—could that ever be hers? Would Thornapple being restored bring happiness like that?

She carefully turned her pillow and tried again to sleep.

Aden could always sleep. Well, almost always. There was the time of the big rain when she'd wakened to see him sitting hunched in the wagon. But that was because he was staying out of the rain and out of her way. And because he was praying. She wondered suddenly what all the man prayed about. From prayers he'd offered aloud, she knew he prayed for his mother, for her parents, and for clients everywhere they'd been. But what did he pray about when no one was listening? Did he pray for her?

A breeze riffled through nearby trees, and Rebekah wished she had a window she could peer from. If it weren't for awakening Aden, she'd climb out and go for a walk. But that was out of the question. She smiled, remembering his cautions about snakes. Wouldn't he be livid if he found her walking in the dark of the night! Aden? Livid? No, that word would never describe Aden. Except—for when she sold Banner—and now he was apologizing for his anger! She would never understand the man.

What made him such a peaceful person? Could it have anything to do with his devotion to God? He would say so, of course. But could it really? Could God really make such a difference in a person's life? Or was he born that way? She thought she'd talk to Betsy Mayfield tomorrow and see what she believed about God. It wouldn't hurt to find out a little more from a nonthreatening source.

But she couldn't let anything change her priorities. It was all right to dream and wonder a bit, but in the end, no matter what, she was going back to Thornapple by Christmas. And if she began to feel the least bit guilty about Aden Robards being so good to her, she must keep reminding herself that, after all, he only married her because her name was Rebekah.

nine.

The smell of wood smoke and coffee boiling brought Rebekah sitting up, scrambling for her clothes. She'd hoped to be the first one up, but that was very hard to accomplish around Aden Robards. She dressed quickly, pleased at her progress in learning how to pull out of a nightgown and into a day dress in the small, trembly wagon. When she brushed her hair, she had to be careful not to hit the side of the wagon; it was so small.

"Smells good," she said as she hopped down. She was determined she'd be cheerful today but keep a comfortable distance, too. "Do we start work in Cornelia today?"

"I'm going to go in and check it out. You can stay here or maybe visit the Mayfields."

"What if you get customers right to begin with? You won't have anyone to assist you."

"No. But I'll manage. What about camping here? Would you like to stay here? Or be closer to town?"

She eyed him over her coffee cup. He really did want to know her choice! She lowered her cup without even drinking. "I like it here," she said, looking about her at the young sturdy trees growing close to stout parents, the stream laced on either side by moss and ferns and giving off a delicate gray vapor. "Let's stay here," she said and smiled at the flush of pleasure that filled his face. "If you wanted to stay here, why bother to ask me?"

"Because it matters what you think—very much," he said.

Her heart did a weird flip, and to be sure he didn't notice anything different about her, she took a big swallow of coffee. The coffee was scalding hot, so she burned her tongue unmercifully. He looked at her and raised one eyebrow, then shook his head—whether in commiseration or condescension, she wasn't sure.

After breakfast Rebekah washed the dishes in the stream while Aden packed his saddlebags with all he thought he'd need of instruments and supplies so the wagon could stay put. After he left, she surveyed the oak thicket, the appled hillside toward the house, sunshine twinkling on dewy grass, a cow mooing on the other side of the fence. She bit the corner of her mouth in indecision. What would she do today? She was first tempted to go for a long walk, maybe for miles, by herself. But she did want to see the Mayfields, and there might not be many days like this. Perhaps Betsy would even let her make bread. She couldn't wait to feel pliable, elastic dough responding to her hands, the smell of warm yeast as the bread rose and baked.

She struck out walking toward the house the way they'd come the night before, following the fence. At the first stout corner post, Rebekah climbed over, managing quite nicely without hanging her skirt up the first time.

The minute she crested the hill, she heard a shrill, happy voice. "Mama says would you like to come help churn." There came Cerise, her brown-red hair today done up neatly in pigtails glistening brightly to go with her snaggle-toothed smile.

Rebekah couldn't restrain a giggle. "How many does it take to churn? Do we all get a turn?"

Cerise grabbed her by the hand and tugged her toward the house. "Everybody who wants to has a turn, and we all try to figure out when the butter's coming so we get to yell 'Butter's here!' first before anyone else."

"And then what happens?" Rebekah smiled down at the little bouncy girl now swinging hands with her.

"Well, you go around feeling smug and pretty all day 'cause you're the Butter Girl," answered Cerise, removing her hand to pose, shoulders back, chin up, one hand on her hip, the other extended, perhaps to appear like a ballet dancer, but appearing more like the spout on a coffee pot, and all the time a silly smile pasted across her face.

Rebekah laughed until they reached the orchard, but the minute she walked under those loaded trees row on row, she felt a hush come over her.

"Why'd you get so quiet all of a sudden? You missing your nice husband?" asked Cerise. "He went to work without you, didn't he?"

"No, no. I mean, yes, he did. But that's not why I got quiet just now. It's these trees. Hear the wind in the leaves? It's—almost as if they're talking."

"Yeah. Sort of, I guess." Cerise kicked at a dry cow pile. "I think it's God talking. That whispery sound, you know? Do you think that's silly?"

"No. Tell me what you mean."

"Just that. God's talking. People are always saying God told them this and God told them that. But He don't ever talk to me like that. But out here"—she waved her hand—"out here I can hear Him talking."

"Well, then. What's He saying?"

"Oh, I don't know that. Not yet. But I don't understand preachers or much of the Bible yet either. I will when I'm older. I guess right now I just know He loves me. More than even my ma and pa do. I can hear that part. Listen real good, and you can hear it, too."

They stood still between the trees with the wind blowing Rebekah's skirt and lifting loose strands of her hair even as it played in the apple leaves.

"Do you hear Him?" asked Cerise in a whisper.

"No, not—not exactly," answered Rebekah. "But I like it. I like it a lot. I've always liked trees—and wind in the leaves."

"Come on—we'd better hurry, or we're gonna hear 'em yellin' 'Butter's here,' an' we won't even get a turn! Can you run? Come on!"

Rebekah took the paddle just in time to become the Butter

Girl. As all the girls, including Betsy, clamored around her, faces bright, voices strong, she knew she'd never had more fun.

Betsy Mayfield washed the butter, working it around and around with a wide spatula in a big wooden bowl until she'd washed all the white buttermilk away, and only occasional cold water beads remained. Then each one tasted buttered bread and passed judgment on its quality. Finally she sent everyone to help Pa and the boys in the south orchard.

"But what about Rebekah?" asked Cerise, clinging to her new friend.

Betsy laughed as she pushed Cerise toward the door. "Rebekah helps me this time!"

"Ma, you know I need to sew on my new dress," pleaded the oldest girl, Rosemary, a half pout on her lips.

"Oh, all right. Scoot and get to sewing! Now, the rest of you, go help Pa. There's more outdoor jobs than inside this time of year," she explained to Rebekah as the door slapped behind giggles and complaints of five girls. Cerise stuck her head back in with a hopeful plea that maybe she was needed to sweep the floor, but even that Betsy turned down.

At last she and Rebekah were alone, and Rebekah realized the teakettle's contents were simmering and that a brisk fire crackled in the stove, sounds she'd not heard with the girls' voices ringing.

"I could go help in the orchard myself," she offered then. "I don't know much about orchards, but I could learn."

"Maybe next time. I was hoping for now that you'd stay with me. I—just get hungry sometimes to know what's going on in other places. Thought maybe you'd tell me something about travels with a dentist. Mind you, I wouldn't like leaving my kitchen behind, but—it does seem pretty exciting, too, waking up in so many different places. I wonder—do you hear mourning doves calling and blue jays fussing everywhere you go? Or maybe some strange birds I've never heard of?"

All this time the short, wide woman was stretching up to

snag a huge pan from its nail, scooping flour into a rusty sifter, busily preparing to make bread.

"Could I—please do that?" asked Rebekah when finally an opening came in Betsy's chatter. "I would love to make a batch of bread more than—almost anything."

"Well, of course. Sure you can. You should have told me. Here I was, blathering on like a windmill on a March day. Sure, Honey, you make bread, an' I'll wash some apples and start getting them cut for pies. But can you talk whilst you work? Maybe you could tell me what it was like in Macon? I've never been south of Commerce. Now Commerce is a good town if you want to buy or sell farm goods, which most everyone in these parts does. But if you want to sit properly and listen to a concert—oh, my goodness, here I go again. Talk, Rebekah, please—I want to hear."

Rebekah sifted mountains of flour, then scooped up a handful of lard and mixed it in with a small crock of yeasty water. The feel of the sticky dough developing soothed an unsettled place in her inner self. She began to fulfill Betsy's request by telling her about the Sharps and then Mrs. Leavenworth and even a little about Banner. Rebekah mixed, and Betsy cut apples; one was happy talking, and the other, for once, happy listening. And the sunshine cast shadows of oak leaves on the plank floor at their feet, and a cat full of spilled cream from the churning slept with her eyes half open underneath the stove.

When she covered the dough for rising, Rebekah washed in a pan in front of a window, dried on a flour sacking cloth conveniently hung on a near nail, then sat down by her new friend, idly pulling the cloth back and forth through her hands.

"Everywhere we go we meet new friends and then leave them," she said, watching Betsy dig in her pan for any apples she'd failed to cut. "That's the hard part."

"Do you go to church, you and Dr. Robards?" asked Betsy, cutting the last apple crisply in half.

"Oh, yes. He would have it no other way."

"And you?"

"Well, I've always gone to church, too."

"But not because you wanted to?"

"I didn't say that." Rebekah suddenly felt she was being interrogated.

"I'm sorry. It just sounded that way. I know Jesus joy when I hear it, and I didn't think I heard it in your response. Now it wouldn't have to be only in church, of course. My, my, we have more Jesus joy right here in this house than would fit in the grandest cathedral. Tell me about your parents and where you grew up—that is, if you don't mind. I–I know I'm too curious, but—please tell me."

Betsy was so guileless, so eager, and her eyes sparkled with anticipation like dark brook pebbles. Rebekah forgot her own momentary irritation and plunged into telling about life at Thornapple. She was stumbling some in trying to explain what happened to Thornapple, about Josh and even about Aden, when the girls' voices could be heard approaching. Maybe she'd tell her about Mother some other time.

"Sounds like a flock of geese, don't it?" said Betsy with a smile and a wink. "Families"—she set the lid back on a large pot of beans and slid a bacon grease can to the back of the stove—"families can get closer or more scattered when troubles come. Will you tell me more, Honey, when you feel like it—and when we have a chance to put sentences together in some kind of peace?"

"Yes. And thank you," answered Rebekah.

"Thank you for what?" demanded Cerise, looking up at Rebekah with her hands on her hips, eyes wide, hair sweaty and matted at the edges of her face.

"Never mind what," said Betsy. "Wash up, girls, and start buzzing. Cerise, go call Rosemary. I declare I forgot about her in there sewing all this time. She must 'a been making basting stitches by hand. Carol, you set the table. Set a plate for

Rebekah, too. Eliza, pour buttermilk. Lucy, you make a pan of gravy—can't anyone do it like you. Fanny, you mash the taters."

"And what about me?" asked Rebekah, finding herself trying to be little to stay out of the traffic. "If I'm eating, then surely I can help."

"Oh. Your bread's ready to make into loaves. Then you can split those leftover biscuits and heat 'em for now. We'll have your good, fresh bread tonight."

After dinner Cerise begged to help Rebekah back to camp since she was loaded with a plate of pie, a patty of butter, and a bowl of beans.

"You will utterly and completely spoil us," Rebekah fussed.

"Everyone needs some spoiling now and then" was Betsy's answer, and David Mayfield rumbled a hearty "Amen" as he held the door for her.

After Cerise had left her and Rebekah was puttering about the camp, reliving the lively day, she realized she hadn't asked Betsy about religion even though she'd had that good opportunity when they were talking about church. Why hadn't she asked? Something about it made her uncomfortable. Yet she really wanted to know. There had to be something to this "Jesus joy," as Betsy Mayfield called it.

Aden had found a good reception for practicing dentistry at Moffatt's Drug Store. Mr. Moffatt, as David Mayfield had told them, was his brother-in-law and had accommodated a dentist two years before. He knew what it would take to make a comfortable corner for waiting clients, as well as a curtained area for the "painful procedures," as he called them.

"What did you find to occupy yourself with?" asked Aden as they sat around the fire after a supper of Betsy's delicious offerings. Huddling around the fire helped keep the mosquitoes away.

"I helped churn at the Mayfields'," she said, smiling as she remembered what fun it was. "I even got to be the Butter Girl for today."

"Oh, my. What's that?"

"It just means I was the one churning when the butter came in. The Mayfields celebrate everything. They have—" She was about to say they had "Jesus joy" but thought better of starting such a conversation with Aden. He was thinking about other things and didn't even notice she'd stopped midsentence.

"I can tell you had a good time at the Mayfields'," he said after a bit, "so I hate to spoil your fun."

"But what?" What had he discovered now?

"But you'd best go with me tomorrow. I'm expecting several clients. One lady is bringing her three children, all with bad teeth."

"Well, you know I really don't—"

"You won't have to go every day," said Aden abruptly, standing suddenly and walking off into the dark.

Rebekah bit her lip. She'd meant to say she didn't mind going, and instead he thought she meant she didn't want to go. Well, the nerve of him to interrupt her and jump to conclusions. She made sure she was in the wagon tucked in for the night when he returned.

ջ

Breakfast done, Rebekah took her time washing dishes in the edge of the stream, turning them upside down to dry on a flat rock she'd leveled like a table. Then Aden called so impatiently, she almost jerked a knot in her neck.

"What did you say?" she called back.

"Why are you taking so long cleaning up?"

"Well, you haven't even hitched up the wagon," she answered, her exasperation clear in her voice.

"We're riding in on horseback as I did yesterday," he explained in a voice of forced calm. "I told you last night the things I took yesterday are all I need for now since Mr. Moffatt has a chair that will do quite nicely and a dry sink we can use."

"I suppose I was asleep when you told me," said Rebekah, walking up from the creek as she dried her hands. "How can

I ever make it up to you?"

He chuckled. "Pretty good, Rebekah. We almost had an argument. Time was when I couldn't get you to talk one bit."

She felt her face flame in indignation. "I'm glad we're riding horseback so I won't have to sit beside you!" she retorted.

❧

It was nice having the wagon in camp whenever Aden decided Rebekah could stay "home" and do laundry. She could also then count her money and consider how she would get home to Thornapple and what she would do once she got there.

It was also nice to have the camp set up so the Mayfield girls could visit her, particularly Cerise. If the wagon hadn't been there, little else would've been, only a pot of grease suspended from a high limb and maybe a couple of bowls and cups drying on Rebekah's flat rock by the stream. And of course smoldering remains of a breakfast fire. Cerise loved to climb inside the wagon and pretend she was going west to Oklahoma. Or she'd climb on a large, gray tree stump on the other side of the stream and use it as her stage for delivering resounding speeches that ended in spastic giggles. Rebekah wondered if there ever in this world had been a more interesting child. Once or twice as she watched Cerise's bare brown feet twinkling with speed as she disappeared over the hill toward home, she allowed herself to wish she could someday be a mother. But it was only once or twice and only for the flash of a second.

Rebekah visited Butterfly Meadows whenever she could. Betsy Mayfield made her feel wanted, even needed, always asking her to tell her about things in the "outside world." Betsy would often arrange it so that for at least a few minutes, she and Rebekah would have the kitchen to themselves, or the porch where they shelled peas, or the garden while picking cucumbers. Rebekah became so comfortable with Betsy that one day she launched into an explanation of how she came to marry Aden, all about the Isaac and Rebekah thing, even how she didn't love him, married him because she didn't know what else to do.

Betsy stopped in the middle of a pod of peas and just listened.

"I don't think I would have been that brave," she said quietly when Rebekah seemed through. "And are you—in love with him now?"

"Oh, no." Rebekah shelled even faster and didn't look up. "I told him I'd ride with him and help him, but I wouldn't really be married to him. I'm going back to Thornapple before Christmas."

"You are?" For the first time Betsy sounded shocked.

Rebekah looked up. "You think I'm terrible, don't you? But, remember, he only married me because of my name. And what kind of a reason is that?"

"My dear, anybody can look at you two and see that Isaac, Aden, whatever his name is, did not marry you only for your name."

"But how? Of course he did! That's what he told me! Only—I've always thought there must be something devious about it, because of course it didn't make any sense."

"Love doesn't make any sense," said Betsy, resting her hands on the side of her bowl and smiling at Rebekah.

"Love? He doesn't love me!" Rebekah's eyes widened in alarm.

Betsy laughed in delight. "Honey, you're in for some marvelous surprises. You aren't always going to be so unhappy."

"I didn't say I wasn't happy."

"But you aren't. And I wish happiness for you. No, better than that, I wish for you to have Jesus joy."

Rebekah smiled at Betsy's oft-used phrase. "I'll be fine once I get back to Thornapple. And I am going back. But I sure will miss all of you. You are a wonderful family. Especially you—and Cerise. But I haven't left yet. And— uhm—Betsy, if you don't mind, don't mention my leaving to

Aden. I'd rather—tell him myself when the time comes."

"Oh dear," said Betsy sighing. "I don't like secrets very much. But I'll try to be quiet. But, Honey, don't you think—"

"Don't try to change my mind, Betsy. There's no use," said Rebekah firmly. "And now tell me when David and the boys are going to be through adding onto the barn?"

"Oh. They are making a terrific racket down there, aren't they? David says they'll be through by Saturday. He says the Yates apples will be ready to pick on Monday, so he's quitting even if he's not quite done. It will be nice having the added storage room."

They were interrupted then by high shrill voices as Lucy and Rosemary hashed out a problem with Lucy's dress fitting. Rosemary could not get Lucy to stand still long enough for her to get the hem straight, and Lucy was furious because Rosemary wouldn't get through so she could go on about her business. Betsy smiled as they ran onto the porch pointing fingers at each other. "Tsk, tsk," she scolded. "Almost grown and still fussing like babies. Both of you, hush. Go take water to your brothers, Lucy, and Rosemary, work on sewing those new curtains until Lucy gets back. If she won't stand still then, I'll come in there and hold her in place."

Rosemary grinned sheepishly and retreated. Lucy scowled and stepped over to the well to draw water.

❧

"I do believe the Mayfields are pretty fond of you," remarked Aden to Rebekah one day as they walked home after one of Betsy's suppers.

"And of you, too," she answered, looking up at him with one of her rare, sweet smiles that gave Aden a thrill of hope. At moments like those, he could believe all animosity was being soaked out of her by the love and kindness of the Mayfield family.

The Moffatts at the drugstore were also very fond of Aden and Rebekah. They insisted on sharing dinner with them at noon whenever they were in the store. Mrs. Moffatt said she didn't know how to cook in small amounts, and she, being a good deal older than her brother, David Mayfield, had no children left at home. She said they'd be depriving her if they didn't help her eat beans, late squash, stewed potatoes, cornbread, and whatever else she'd "thrown together."

They were all eating together on September 20, the four of them, as well as Sheriff Bozeman and his chess-playing buddy Raeford Banks. The sheriff had himself removed the chess game from a mottled table when ordered to by Mrs. Moffatt, who said she wouldn't dare touch it. The sheriff had tenderly placed the chess set beside a golden hoop of cheese on Moffatt's scarred counter and was making some joke about whether cheese and chess made compatible companions, when Mr. Baggett from down at the depot came rushing in, his few hairs all awry, his glasses about to fall off. He was waving a telegram and so breathless it was hard to understand him.

Not realizing the seriousness of Mr. Baggett's message, Mrs. Moffatt continued her stream of dinner preparation remarks as she, with Rebekah's help, set food on the table.

"Mother, will you hush and listen to this man?" demanded Mr. Moffatt sternly.

"Well, of course I will," said Mrs. Moffatt, blushing right up to her ears and setting down a pot of beans with a plunk.

"Now. What did you say, Baggett?" asked Mr. Moffatt.

The man gasped for air, and Rebekah wondered if he were about to have some kind of attack. Then the news came out.

"President's—dead. Died—yesterday. Says it right here. From the bullet he took July 2 in Washington."

"Oh dear!" whispered Mrs. Moffatt, edging up beside her husband as if suddenly seeking safety or maybe to offer sympathy.

"I thought he was getting better," said Mr. Moffatt dully.

The sheriff walked back over to his chess game and very

methodically began putting the pieces into a grimy wooden box, pawns first, then rooks, knights, bishops, and finally the king and queen. Rebekah wanted to cry, as Mrs. Moffatt was starting to do, but instead she felt wooden herself like one of the sheriff's pawns. She looked at Aden and wasn't surprised to see he had bowed his head.

They stayed on at the drugstore for a couple of hours, but no one even thought about teeth at a time like this. Aden and Rebekah were part of the growing crowd simply sitting and standing about saying the same things over and over, about poor Mrs. Garfield and all those children; about what could make a person, no matter how disgruntled, do such a horrible thing; about how Abraham Lincoln was a Republican, too. Rebekah was very glad when Aden said they might as well go home.

Of course they went directly to the Mayfields in case they hadn't heard. They found David Mayfield in the orchard, and he immediately began hobbling toward the house, calling everyone to come with him. They all gathered, not in the kitchen, but for this solemn occasion in the room that served as dining room and bedroom and, as now, parlor.

"I can't believe it," said Betsy.

"I know. We all thought that of course he'd get well. He just had to," said Rebekah.

David sat hunched forward, elbows on knees, dirty field hat still in his hands. His mouth worked with emotion. "We lost a president already in '65. Didn't hold with all his views, but he was my president. Just like Mr. Garfield. What's our country comin' to? You children, you listen to me. There won't never be a time you won't remember this day, where you was, what you was doin' when you heard the news. And whenever you remember this day, you remember your ol' daddy tellin' you—tellin' you firm—that God is greater than all this. He's greater, you hear me? That assassin thinks he's won, but he ain't won." His voice shook, and he reached to a back pocket to drag out a handkerchief. Betsy Mayfield laid a rough hand on his shoulder and gently massaged it.

Rebekah wondered if her own father knew about this. Surely he would by now. He kept up with everything so carefully. She imagined that he would be pretty angry with the assassin and very solemn, even stunned. But she certainly couldn't picture him stopping to pray about it as Aden had or preaching a sermon like David. Everyone was so different.

But no matter how stunning the news or how it might seem that life would never be normal again, it actually didn't take long for everyone to pick up their tools and get back to work. The cows didn't know a president had died. The horses still needed feeding. Apples were steadily ripening, many Yateses were ready to pick, and sweet crisp Terries would be ripe in a week or two. Shockleys wouldn't be ready till later. One last field of corn begged to be harvested. Aden didn't do any more dental work that week except for those who came pleading for relief from a toothache. He and Rebekah helped pick apples for a few days, and each day one could feel a little more relief from the awesomeness of what had happened. The Cotton Expo would still happen. Life would go on. The new president, Mr. Chester Arthur, must know what he was doing. The United States was too great to be halted by one assassin, no matter how devastating his work.

One morning after Aden and Rebekah had resumed their usual schedule, he assured her he wouldn't need her that day, told her she could visit and help out at Butterfly Meadows. She didn't argue with him and almost forgot there was sadness anywhere, so caught up she became in the merriment of the big working family. As it came time to go build a fire at camp and get ready for Aden's return, she determined that this time she would graciously turn down all Betsy's offerings of bacon, fresh bread, butter, and buttermilk. But she wasn't prepared for refusing the offer Betsy came up with that day.

"I know you must have your own Bible, Honey," said

Betsy, wiping her hands on her apron pockets before sliding a
book carefully from a little shelf near the big breakfast table.
"I guess you don't need another Bible. But—because I've
come to love you so, I really want you to have this particular
Bible. It was my uncle Longstreet's. He didn't mind making
notes in the margins, underlining, and even, in some places,
circling certain words that excited him." She pushed the Bible
gently into Rebekah's hands as she watched her face.

"I–I don't know—"

"You don't have to know all about the Author to understand
His words," said Betsy. "Read at least Genesis and Exodus.
You'll find the stories about Isaac and Rebekah there, you
know. And—oh, let me see it again for a minute—" She took
the book and, lifting one knee to make a temporary table,
licked a finger and flipped pages. "Here—be sure and read all
the Gospel of John. Don't miss that. And, of course, one of my
favorite books is right here in the middle—Psalms. But here I
go, telling you too much. You will take it, won't you?"

Betsy laid the book back in her hands as if it were a gen-
uine pearl laid out on dark velvet. There was no way to
refuse what this lady with the sparkling brown eyes was asking her to do.

"Sure. I'll read—"

"When business is slow?"

"Yes. Thank you, Betsy. You are so good to me."

"I feel as if we're kin—somehow," said Betsy with a
laugh, turning to the stove to check on a kettle of apples.

She knew she wouldn't read in front of Aden and bring on
his questions. That limited when she would fill this Betsy
assignment, but she'd do it somehow.

And it wasn't hard, once she got started. She couldn't
believe she'd ever thought Genesis was dull reading. It was
chock full of stories, colorful stories. She read and reread the
tales of Abraham, his precious son Isaac whom he was willing to sacrifice but didn't have to after all, and then Isaac and

his Rebekah, the girl from "back home." She read all about Moses and the rescuing of God's enslaved people. She read John and memorized some verses that Uncle Longstreet had marked so she had to see them every time she opened the Bible. She puzzled and pondered those words about being condemned just for not accepting God, yet being saved eternally by trusting in Jesus, His Son. Then one day as light was failing and Aden was busy collecting fresh firewood, she sat by a beech tree where roots made a perfect seat near the stream, and she read Psalm 23 until it became part of her. She knew Mother treasured those words, though she hadn't talked a lot about them. She'd heard her mumbling, "The Lord is my shepherd," when she didn't know Rebekah was listening. And now as she read the words over and over, the word *shepherd* began to take on a new meaning. What if all this about God's caring for one's daily needs were true? What if one could "dwell in the house of the Lord forever"? She wanted to talk to Aden about it, but somehow the moment was never quite right. He seemed so detached and worried these days. He still read to her from his Bible after breakfast each morning, but he no longer expected any response from her.

She began to pray every day in her own awkward way that she would somehow understand what God expected of her, that she would know what she must do in order to have the "Jesus joy" Betsy Mayfield talked about and the peace she'd recognized in Isaac Aden Robards. She didn't know what to expect, but perhaps a sudden burst of power, an electrical sensation, or something very extraordinary would come. So when the Lord quietly changed her life, she hardly realized it for awhile.

"Lord, I know You're God," she said one day as she washed and sterilized instruments in a back room of Moffatt's Drug Store. "Whatever it takes, Lord, make me Your child because that's what I want to be."

A few days later, she walked through the orchard with Cerise, carrying a jug of milk and tin of cookies to busy apple-pickers.

"This is the best time of year," said Cerise, her long brown hair flipping from side to side as she skipped along.

"Why is this the best? What about Christmas?"

Cerise looked up at her friend and screwed up her face in thought. "Well, Christmas is very, very good. But this is better. We are always so happy when we have a big job to do, and everyone is slaving to get the crop in. It's such a fruity delicious time. I love the smell of apples and everything so lively! I wonder if there's an orchard in heaven. I bet there is."

"But—Cerise, how do you know—how can you be sure you'll be in heaven?"

The little girl stopped in her tracks, looked up at Rebekah with widened eyes so clear and bright. Rebekah caught her breath at their beauty. "Rebekah, I know, I just know, because—I told God I wanted to be His child forever. And that's all it takes."

"That's all it takes? You're sure? There must be something more!"

"No. No more. That's all it takes. Come on! There's Rosemary coming to meet us. She looks done in, doesn't she? She'd a lot rather be sewing than picking." Cerise giggled and ran ahead to meet Rosemary.

Rebekah sighed and took a deep breath. The sky above was bluer than she'd ever seen before at Thornapple or anywhere. Globes of ripe apples glistened among leaves lifting in a feathery breeze. Mayfield voices merrily shouting from tree to tree broke into shouts of glee as they realized milk and cookies had arrived on the scene. Amid the shoving and teasing and squealing, Rebekah started her own celebration.

Lord, I'm really Yours now. I never knew it before, but today, this very day, I know I'm really and truly Yours. Oh, just wait until I tell Betsy!

When Betsy heard the news, she cried and laughed and hugged and cried some more. Then she told the rest, and they all hugged Rebekah, and Cerise squealed happily and said they should every one have an extra serving of pie just for joy.

"Aden will be so excited!" said Betsy, a big smile crinkling her cheeks. "When will you tell him?"

"I—tonight, I guess. Do please let me tell him myself," said Rebekah, suddenly feeling very shy.

But when she tried that night to tell Aden what had happened, her tongue went numb, and he didn't even notice she was attempting to talk. Later, as she lay in the darkened wagon, she tried to sort things out. How long had it been since Aden confided anything in her? Why should she blame him for not recognizing her great need to speak? She wondered if it was right to try to pull back the curtain that seemed to have come between their lives. Maybe it was kinder to leave it the way it was until she left. Was she still leaving? Everything seemed so different now.

ten

David and Lawrence took apples to Commerce periodically when they had enough to warrant the trip. In late September they delivered a nice load of Yateses and Terries and returned talking jubilantly about all the activity in that market town.

Aden and Rebekah had supper with the Mayfields that Friday night. Aden, David, Lawrence, and Freddie all went out on the porch while the women and girls cleared the table and washed up. Rebekah heard a rumble of thunder and wondered whether Aden would think they needed to put Jake and Jolly in the Mayfields' barn. Then she forgot about the horses as Rosemary described dramatically how Luke Stoker had looked as he swaggered into school in full Indian dress that day.

"He's so proud of being an Indian that he wants everyone to know. Some people, Jack Tulley for one, think Luke's plum weird. But I think—well, it's really romantic."

"Especially since Luke is so, so handsome!" said Lucy, laughing as she swiped a towel against Rosemary's back.

Suddenly Aden's tall figure filled the doorway. "Storm's coming, Rebekah. We need to batten down. Wouldn't want our little wagon to blow away," he said with a chuckle to Betsy Mayfield.

"Well, we don't want you two to blow away either," said David Mayfield, limping as he followed Aden inside. "Now we've got plenty of room. You go bring your horses, wagon, and all to the barn, and then come spread out in the parlor. It's all yours. If our children rob you of your privacy, I'll rob them of an ear or two."

"Oh, no, we'll be fine. It's only going to be a quick blow

135

and then over," said Aden. Then he looked at Rebekah. "Of course if you'd rather stay here—"

"No, I'll go help," she said quickly. "Let's go! Thank you for the delicious supper," she called as they crossed the porch.

The rain came in deluges before they even got to the wagon. Aden shouted at Rebekah to get in the wagon, and she didn't bother to say she wouldn't. But while he tied ropes to the wagon wheels and secured them around nearby oak saplings, she rounded up Jake and Jolly and tethered them close by. She got in the wagon and was mopping water out of her eyes and drying her hair on a towel when Aden tumbled in.

The wagon shook as if a giant had it in his fist, shaking it to hear it rattle. Thunder blasted behind burst after crackling streak of lightning. Rebekah tossed her damp towel to the dark shape of Aden.

He caught the towel neatly. "Guess we're kind of in for it," he said.

"Not for the first time," she reminded him.

There was no chance to talk after that. The storm was too terrific. Rebekah knew Aden was praying, and now she could pray, too. What was it he'd said before? God was showing off—that was it. She tried to relax and enjoy the show, but she wished she could be more of a spectator and less involved in the storm's anger and fury. She kept thinking the canvas must be ripped off and several times reached out to touch it to be sure it was still there.

Suddenly she felt Aden's hand close around hers. He gripped her hand so hard, the bones were crushed against each other. She held onto him as if he were the only plank on a stormy sea. She couldn't help but think, too, how nice and warm his big, hard hand was. They were still clinging to each other when the torrent suddenly lightened to abrupt bursts and abatements, as if the Mayfield girls were throwing buckets of water against them but couldn't keep up.

Aden let go of her hand and crawled to the opening. Even

in its calmer state, the storm drowned out anything they tried to say. Aden peered out from time to time, and Rebekah was sure he was worrying about the horses. Finally she felt the wagon pitch as he jumped to the ground. She pulled a blanket close around her shoulders and sighed from relief that all was well. They should really have been up at the Mayfields', but there hadn't been time, and as it was, she wasn't sorry she'd stayed with Aden. She laid her hand against her cheek and whispered to herself, "If only we could start over."

Aden's shout shook her out of her reverie. What could be wrong now? It must be Jake or Jolly. As soon as she looked out of the opening, she knew it wasn't the horses. Fire! *The Mayfields' house?*

"I can't tell whether it's the house or the barn!" yelled Aden, running toward the fence.

Without any consideration whatsoever, she ran after him.

Realizing as soon as she crested the hill that it was actually the barn on fire, Rebekah allowed herself to slow up momentarily, then plowed on again, her wet skirts clinging to her legs, her feet heavy in soggy grass. How could a barn burn down in a pouring rain? Hearing Cerise screaming, Rebekah forced her feet to go faster through the sodden grass. Now she heard horses neighing and David yelling to his boys not to run in, that he'd do it himself. As Rebekah arrived finally in the barnyard, the first person she noticed was Betsy with her hair all down and flying about her red face as she threw futile buckets of water into the flames. Everything shone garishly, lit by an orange holocaust. Nothing seemed real. Rebekah staggered against a sturdy hitching post to catch her breath. Out of the shadows Cerise came flying to her, her long nightgown wadded up around her knees so she could run.

"Aden's in there!" she cried, pointing at what appeared to be nothing but flaming walls.

Rebekah lunged forward, but Lucy was suddenly there wrapping thin arms around her. "No, Rebekah!" she yelled in her ear. "You can't go, too!"

Out of the hungry flames thundered the horses, crazy with fear. Their neighs were more like screams as they ran blindly away from the fire. Betsy threw down her bucket and snatched Cerise to her as one of the mules with nostrils flared reared up momentarily, then crashed away into the rainy darkness. One horse's mane was on fire, but it ran around wildly in a tight circle, and no one could get hold of it. At last, David ripped his own wet shirt off and managed after a couple of tries to throw it over the horse's head. He and Lawrence together smothered the flame, and the smell of scorched hair made Cerise gag. But Rebekah hardly noticed, because she was straining to see Aden come out, now that the horses were free. What had happened to him? Why didn't he come on?

"Go in and pull Aden out! Pull him out!" screamed Rebekah, but she barely heard her own voice because of the roar of the flames and the confusion of horses and people.

Then she felt strong arms come around her from behind. Just as she tried to break free, she heard Aden's voice next to her ear and turned to collapse against his smoky body.

"It's all right, Rebekah," he repeated in a soothing voice as she wept against his neck.

"But I didn't know where you were," she babbled.

"Well, I hardly did either," he said, tucking strands of wet hair behind her ear. "But God knew where I was. I found an opening at the back and ran out there after I released the horses. There now, we're all going to be all right."

"Thank God!" she whispered into his collar.

"Aden, help!" cried Lawrence. "There's a horse down over here behind the woodshed. I think her leg's broken!"

Rebekah felt him squeeze her tightly then set her aside. She clung to him unreasonably, but he pushed her out of the way so he could respond to Lawrence's call. She felt suddenly bereft and couldn't imagine why she was shaking so, she who always had taken farm tragedies in stride, whose father had depended on her never to panic in a crisis. What had gotten into her? What a fool she'd made of herself!

She shuddered, hugging herself in chill dampness, even as her cheeks burned from the fire's intense heat. Cerise slipped up beside her, and she circled the child in her arms, wishing she knew what to say or do. She felt more than heard deep sobs of the child, and she squeezed her harder, holding her face against her chest so she wouldn't have to see the horrible fire or the writhing horse surrounded by men, one with a rifle. But Cerise pulled away enough to swipe at her tears and then look again at the awesome sight of the barn's skeleton in flames, falling one large piece at a time. At the gun's explosion, the little girl piled into Rebekah again, and they wept together, their warm tears absorbed into the cold rain.

When the rain slowed to a drizzle and the wind quieted, the fire still burned. There was nothing to do but watch. In the end, some charred timbers were left, even a few upright studs, and one entire corner, the new storage room. David Mayfield said he wished it would every bit burn while it was about it, making the cleanup easier. Being new wood, it had not burned as completely as the rest but was certainly no longer useful. The smell of roasting apples mingled with those of scorching hay and wood smoke.

"Good thing we took as many apples as we did to market on Wednesday," said David.

Someone asked how the barn could have burned in such a downpour.

"It was a tinderbox, a grip of splinters ready to be torched," explained David calmly. "My father built this barn in 1835, built it first, before the house, and made it proud and sturdy of heart pine. He bragged many a time on that barn, said it was his aim to give his animals a palace, just what they deserved for all their hard work." David grinned at the memory, then stroked his chin thoughtfully. "Guess I've got my work cut out for me, boys, trying to replace that old barn."

Betsy eased up beside her man, and he looped an arm around her neck, drawing her close. "We can do it, can't we, Betsy girl?" he asked as he tried to wipe smut from her nose and only added more to it.

"We'll build it even better," she answered. "Maybe even have a neat corner for my quilting frame."

"Oh dear, now she's gone to meddlin'," said David, giving her a little shake.

Rebekah glanced furtively at Aden standing alone several feet away. He hadn't come back to her after dealing with the horse. Would she have pushed him away if he had? She really didn't know. It was a strange night, and comfort was so important. He had held her hand in the storm and had hugged her during the fire. But it was just part of his generous, protective nature. That was all. She watched him now, standing with his feet apart as if ready to spring into action, his hands fisted at his sides. What was he thinking? She could see only his profile in the flickering yellow light.

The rain had all but stopped, and there was no more thunder, though streaks of lightning still snapped ragged rips in the sky. Freddie commented with some sort of joy that Lucy looked like a drowned rat who'd been digging in a coal bin. Carol took up for Lucy by accusing Freddie of having "near 'bout" half his hair singed off. Betsy shushed them and declared she was going to put on a big pot of coffee. As she bustled away, she threw orders over her shoulder: for Rosemary to stop moping and come serve some apple pie; for Carol to stack the buckets up and put them back by the well; for Cerise to stop pulling on Rebekah's braid and make herself useful in the kitchen.

Cerise looked up at Rebekah as if she expected some sort of defense. Rebekah nudged the little girl forward and said she'd help, too.

A number of neighbors had arrived at various stages and

now happily took part in Betsy's refreshments, almost as if it were a party. Mrs. Banks had brought a pot of coffee herself, sure that the men would need to watch all night. And Mrs. Carey brought half a pound cake, apologizing that if she'd known they'd have this fire, she wouldn't have let the family devour the first half at supper.

It was after midnight when Betsy insisted that Rebekah come on to bed with her girls since it was obvious Aden was not going to leave the scene.

As they walked toward the house, Betsy told Rebekah in a consoling tone that men believed they had to fix whatever happened—it was part of their makeup—and that, anyway, not a one of them would want to leave until the rest did, something of a competition thing. "And, of course, your Aden was a wonder tonight saving our horses. We'll always remember that."

"He was a hero," said Rosemary dreamily, holding the door for Rebekah.

The memories of that night would always bring forth scents of acrid smoke and then the overpowering pleasantness of Betsy's smooth sage soap as Rebekah bathed the greasy blackness from her face and hands.

Rosemary and Rebekah shared a bed with Carol and Lucy, who both went to sleep promptly. The night reminded Rebekah somehow of times months ago at the Sharps'. It rained so much then, too, and she bunked up with their children. But at that time she was so glad she didn't have to share the wagon with Aden. And now she missed him, wished she could talk to him. The two younger girls, after some arguing, had agreed that Rebekah and Rosemary should have the coveted outside spots in the overfull bed. Now, out of the darkness on the other side of the bed, Rosemary spoke in a whisper, "You have such a handsome husband. Even when he's covered with grime and grit he's so very—" She left her sentence hanging, obviously unable to think of a word that would adequately express her admiration.

Rebekah turned her face toward her, considered what to reply, but never got it out before she was sure Rosemary was asleep. He was handsome and good and a hero, all those things. But he wasn't really her husband.

৯

It took several days for the piles of burned tin and other rubble to cool enough for safe removal. But when David Mayfield put the word out that he was clearing the charred barn, getting ready to build again, Aden was there to help the very next day. Rebekah never knew whether he contacted Mr. Moffatt to cancel that day's appointments or just what he did. She stayed busy helping cook for all the workers, including other neighbors who came to help. But when she crawled into her bed in the wagon, her mind foggy with weariness, she had time to wonder at what was going on in her heart. For instance, why had Aden become so quiet, and why did he no longer try to talk to her? Why had he hugged her so tenderly the night of the fire but now had nothing to say? Had he finally given up? And if he had, wasn't that just what she'd wanted all these months? So why did she have such a dull heartsick feeling in the pit of her stomach?

They still had apples to pick, too. Every apple she picked, Rebekah felt, was a gift saved from the fire. She found that aside from cooking for the workers, she could do little to help with the barn. And often Aden insisted he didn't need her to assist him if all he had scheduled were tooth pullings. So she picked apples.

It was while Rebekah was picking small, hard Terry apples one day that she got to thinking about all that money saved up for buying a piece of Thornapple. It wasn't hers. How had she dared to steal from a man who had rescued her from becoming a charity case? Oh, he said it was because her name was Rebekah, but that couldn't possibly be it, of course. And now that she had a clearer perspective on it all, now that she was looking at all that had happened with eyes

Jesus had opened, she saw that Isaac Aden Robards had simply not been able to walk away without helping her. And he had made it clear that he was intending to marry her for keeps. It was she who had insisted on a marriage of convenience. And how had she thanked him? By robbing him over and over again! She felt a wave of nausea and gripped the top of her ladder for support.

"You okay up there, Rebekah?" called Carol from the next tree.

"I'm fine. Just got a bit hot, I guess," she said.

"Maybe you better get some water. There's plenty in a jug at the end of the next row. Some cold biscuits and jam, too. Mama believes in keeping her slaves well fed."

"Did someone say biscuits and jam?" yelled Lucy, emptying her bulging apple sack into a crate.

"Oh, Lucy, you eat almost as much as Lawrence! How can you possibly stay so skinny?" asked Carol, adjusting her ladder so she could reach more apples.

"I am not skinny!" declared Lucy. "I'm simply trim."

This brought a derisive hoot from all the girls near enough to hear her. The rest of the morning they burst out from time to time with "She's simply trim!" followed by high giggles.

In spite of Carol's suggestion, Rebekah gave herself a little shake and continued working. She wanted to fill her sack before she went for a drink.

She couldn't keep the money. She knew that now. But how was she going to give it back? How could she return several hundred dollars without admitting her guilt? At one time she'd been brazen enough that the thought of being caught only bothered her because she would lose the money she intended to use for Thornapple. Now—what bothered her now was that she'd done wrong. She wanted to make it right. But then Aden would know. Aden would know, and he would hate her. There would be no hope. Hope of what? Well, maybe it was silly. Maybe she'd talked to Betsy so much, she'd caught her romantic enthusiasm and could believe almost anything good. But she had begun to dream, at first unconsciously but now more and more consciously, that she and Aden could be really married. She didn't know how it could happen, but she felt in her soul that it wasn't a bad dream to foster, that Jesus was pleased with dreams such as these. But if Aden discovered her burglary—well, it would be all over then.

Aden had held her hand hard in the storm; he had always been so careful to make her comfortable, had arranged for her to stay inside at the Sharps', and had tried to cover for her so she'd not be embarrassed. Even when she'd been as ornery as she knew how, she'd noticed him taking extra pains to be pleasant, as in shaving his dark whiskers almost every day. Aden had provided her a horse, paid her utter respect as they worked side by side, had said very seriously that what she thought mattered. But over and over again she had rebuffed him. Now—now she knew that what he thought mattered—so very much!

She hadn't told Aden yet what had happened in her life, that she had committed her allegiance to Jesus Christ. She wanted to be sure to tell him when he would wholeheartedly believe her, not think she was trying to please him or butter him up. And she hoped that maybe he would notice the difference. But he hardly seemed to notice her at all anymore, much less see a change in her.

eleven

Aden untied Jake and Jolly from the gray trunk of a stout hickory tree and began to saddle them for their trip into town. Rebekah enjoyed the reflection of his movements in the stream as she washed their bowls.

"That hickory tree is the exact same color as goldenrods, but it looks a lot crisper," she called out.

Aden chuckled. "As if you'd eat either one. Actually, the hickory will be feeding us soon, won't it?" He tightened saddle straps on Jolly and squinted up through the leafy golden foliage. "Nuts will fall soon. Maybe we can have a nut pie for Thanksgiving."

"If the squirrels don't eat them all first," said Rebekah, turning bowls upside down on her flat stone and wiping her hands on her apron.

As they rode to town, they were silent for the most part. But Rebekah felt encouraged that perhaps things were better between them. At least they could enjoy simple conversations about hickory leaves!

They had varying dental cases that day. A Mr. Jenkins had a mouth full of rotten teeth, and he wanted them fixed now that he, a widower, was planning to marry Miss Sophia Jordan. But Mr. Jenkins hated pain, too. Working on him was a trial for the dentist and his assistant. Several other people had simple tooth drawings, and one gentleman wanted Aden to make him a partial device so he could speak without a lisp since he'd lost three front teeth. Aden had to argue with him for awhile before they settled on a plan.

As Rebekah boiled instruments on the Moffatts' back room stove getting ready for the next day, she leaned her forehead against a little, yellow cupboard. Today, as every day, her prayer was that God would show her how to tell Isaac Aden about her theft. She knew now that she must. But how?

Should she boldly bring out the sock full of money and face him with it head on? Or should she cook him a real delicious cake at the Mayfields' and then lead up to the dreaded subject while they sat picnicking by their stream? Or should she ask a mediator, like Betsy, to help her? But that would entail telling Betsy, too, and she couldn't do that!

She was so deep in thought as they rode home that Aden had to speak to her several times before she realized he was talking to her.

"I'm sorry," she said, turning pink with confusion. "I was—trying to figure something out."

He grinned, almost as he used to do at the beginning. "Must be a pretty big project," he said. "If there'd been a snake in your path or anything else to spook Jolly, he'd have dumped you easily."

"So—what did I miss?" she asked.

"Oh. It wasn't that important. I was just saying the Mayfields are about to finish their barn—think they'll be done tomorrow drying in. And—I guess you know about the party tomorrow night."

"Oh—yes! Yes, I do." Her heart gave a leap. "Cerise said there would be dancing."

"That's what David said. He's invited Jess Porter—remember the fellow who ended up on the floor with both of us manhandling him to get his teeth out? He's asked him to bring his fiddle. But that's not all. They're going to have horseshoes to play and some competitions, and of course, plenty of food. I thought—maybe you'd make one of those caramel cakes again. I'm sure Betsy would let you use her oven."

"But—tomorrow's Friday. We don't have appointments?"

"No. I want to help finish that barn," said Aden. "Will you make a cake?"

"Yes! Yes, I will!" She was inordinately pleased. He liked the caramel cake she'd made. He was asking her to do something—for pleasure!

As they rode into camp and she saw the little wagon huddled like a large sitting hen under the trees, a feeling of despair gripped her heart. She could almost *see* that sock leaping out of its hiding place all on its own. How could she go on with this horrible, despicable deed unconfessed, hanging about her like a horrible shroud? Yet—what could she do about it? She'd have to wait now until after the party. She couldn't ruin the nice workday tomorrow and the party. After that she'd tell him, maybe before they even got back to the wagon.

❧

"Rebekah, you're so very quiet today," observed Rosemary as she peeled and chopped fresh turnip roots.

"No need for her to talk when we're jabbering like so many magpies," said Lucy, coming to Rebekah's defense at the same time she glanced at their friend. "But you do look a little pale. Don't you feel well? It's going to be such fun tonight, dancing and all!"

"Oh, I'm perfectly fine," said Rebekah as, for the third time, she sifted flour for her cake. This cake had to turn out scrumptiously light. She wouldn't think about that horrible money. She'd concentrate on this cake. She tossed her braid over her shoulder, hoping at the same time to rid herself of nagging thoughts.

She'd lain awake for miserable hours plotting how she would tell Aden, then had fallen asleep just before dawn. When she awoke, Aden had already gone to work on the barn, so she hadn't seen him alone today—had only come by the merry builders on her way to the house. And merry they were. All signs of that horrific fire were gone except for a dead limb or two on nearby hickory trees and a pile of charred debris removed to the edge of the yard. What one noticed now was the fine new barn smelling of fresh pine lumber. Today the framework was thick with workmen whistling, calling out jokes, mainly working on the roof, which was to be done by nightfall. Even the family's dogs, the whole hassling pack of them, looked happy as if they, too, were part of this energetic project.

A tame fire, so different from that of a few weeks ago, crackled cheerfully between the barn and the house, handy for warming hands on this chilly morning and for burning bits of refuse. Rebekah asked Lawrence why they needed a fire, and he gave those reasons then added one more. "It's just the way we do things," he said, scratching his head as if he himself didn't completely understand. "Unless it's dead heat of summer, we always have a fire when we're building."

"Get Rebekah an iron pan for caramelizing sugar, Cerise," Betsy said. "And all of you stop pestering her about being quiet. No reason, I guess, for her to be as excited about today as we are. And, Cerise, you need to run see if there's any more eggs. I'll be so glad when we have a barn again so those poor hens can figure out where to lay. I declare, we can't keep up with the odd places they find for their nests."

"I know!" laughed Lucy, trimming the edges of a third piecrust. "I found a nest yesterday under the house."

"You did not find it! I did!" declared Cerise.

"I knew it was under there—you were just my envoy to collect the eggs."

"Girls! Who cares who found it as long as we get the eggs? Now scoot, Cerise. We're going to need every egg we can get today, what with pies, Rebekah's cake, potato salad, and whatever else comes up."

"Like maybe some plain boiled eggs for hungry characters like Lawrence," said Lucy. Rolling out leftover piecrust scraps, she cut them into strips and pricked them with a fork. "If that boy comes in this kitchen and sees these homemade crackers before I hide them, they'll be gone before I can draw breath."

"You mean before you can eat them yourself," said Rosemary.

Rebekah let the lively, friendly bantering wash over her. How lovely it would have been to grow up in a family like this. Responsibilities were shared, criticisms were shared, and laughter at everyone and oneself was warmly shared. Immediately she felt guilty for having wished for any childhood other than the one she'd had. Father and Mother had been so good to her. If she'd had six brothers and sisters instead of only one, life would have been considerably different. *But what if they'd all been lazy and troublesome like Josh? Oh, my!* She quickly turned that thought into a prayer for her brother, wherever he might be.

She closed the oven door on her cake and went to work helping Betsy salt and flour pieces of three chickens. Betsy had cut her thumb in the process of dressing and cutting up the chickens, so her progress was impeded. "Stupid thing to do," she fussed now, her right thumb wound up in a piece of flour sacking and sticking up at an awkward angle. "That last bird, crazy thing, was tougher than I expected."

Lawrence and a neighbor, Ben Carey, set up some boards on sawhorses outside the new barn for spreading the feast. Mrs. Carey brought a kettle of chicken and dumplings. Betsy confided in Lucy that if she'd known those dumplings were coming, she wouldn't have cooked that third chicken and could have avoided cutting her thumb. Mrs. Banks brought a great boiler almost full of turnip greens, which was a wonderful addition, and she brought a big pan of cornbread, too.

"I didn't bring any butter since you always seem to have plenty," said Mrs. Banks cheerfully. "Our milk's not very rich about now, for some reason, so we're short of butter."

Betsy nodded and smiled. "Cerise, run and get the butter and bring that big jar of buttermilk, too. Oh, Lucy, go with her. We need those pickles, too. And a few more glasses. Carol, see how many blocks of wood you can roll over for seats. Freddie, you help your sister. Sure do miss the hay about now. But if the barn hadn't burned, we wouldn't be having this workday anyway, would we, so's to need the seats."

They ate so much at noonday, the women had to start all over again cooking for that night. Betsy insisted that Rebekah save her cake for supper. "Tonight's the real party," she said, "an' everything'll be a bit dressier—at least we will. You are going to fix yourself up for tonight, aren't you?"

Rebekah blushed. She hadn't realized she was unkempt, but Betsy's look said she was downright rumpled. "Sure. I'll change," she said.

"Wear that dress that spins, the blue one with a little ruffle around the neck," said Cerise, sucking her finger after taking a pinch of cookie dough.

"But it has short sleeves," said Rebekah.

"Wear a sweater."

"Lucy needs to put your hair up in braids, Cerise. You look a mess yourself," said Carol. Cerise stuck her tongue out at her sister but then grinned, glad she'd have her hair braided.

Rebekah had washed in the stream and was slipping the blue cotton "spin around" dress over her head when she heard Aden's footsteps outside. She jerked the dress down and smoothed it quickly, looked at herself in a small, cracked mirror, and proceeded to undo her braid. It looked as if she'd slept in it about a week. Her fingers felt fumbly as she hurried to get ready. It suddenly seemed so important that he see her looking good.

She heard him washing in the stream and bit a corner of her lower lip. If only, oh, if only that sock full of money would disappear. Maybe she could bury it!

"'Ebekah!" he called at the wagon opening, using her old Molly Sharp nickname. She spun so quickly, she bumped her head then had to laugh at her clumsiness. "Hey!" he said, leaning into the wagon, amusement twinkling in his eyes. "Come here!"

It was amazing how long it took her to cover the distance between that back corner and the flap opening of Aden's tiny wagon. She didn't know what he would do when she got there, but she knew more than anything she wanted to find out.

He put up his hands to help her as she jumped lightly to the ground. His warm hands held her firmly, then, at the waist as he gazed into her face with an insistent light in his blue eyes. Her heart thudded erratically as slowly she placed her own hands on his shoulders. His kiss was so sweet, so tender—and so urgent. "Rebekah!" he whispered against her ear. "I really do love you!"

She pulled away, still keeping her hands on his shoulders. "You—you said—"

"That I love you," he finished for her, moving one hand from her waist to tilt her chin upward with one finger.

"But you can't—I mean, you don't know—" *Oh, what should I do?*

"I'm sorry. I'm being too pushy. You just look so ravishing in that dress. Tell you what—you go on up to the Mayfields' and let me spruce up some. And don't you dare give the first dance away," he ended as he turned her toward the path.

She turned back, determined to tell him all. But the look in his twinkling eyes arrested her. Later. She'd tell him later. They'd have the party first.

"Hi, Rebekah! Don't look so solemn!" said Lawrence as she walked into the barnyard. "My! Don't you look nice! Say, think I could sneak one little piece of that cake before supper? It looks so delicious, and they said you made it."

She laughed, relieved to have her dread and fear dispelled by Lawrence's greed. "No, Lawrence, you may not have even one slice of that cake until you clean up and eat your dinner!" she declared, trying to sound fierce.

"Oh, well!" he said with a shrug. "It was worth a try. All right, I'm going to make myself presentable, as Mama says." He threw a grin over his shoulder as he sauntered off, totally unembarrassed at his failed attempt.

Rebekah had never seen horseshoes played, much less tried the game herself. It was Cerise who demanded, insisted, and pleaded with her until she agreed to play. She fought against disappointment that Aden himself hadn't asked her to play, but then what could she expect? They had hardly been talking to each other for so long, and just because he felt suddenly romantic and kissed her didn't mean he would continue to pay her attention. She wondered if he would remember he'd told her to save him the first dance. Probably not. When she realized partners played from opposite stakes and thus she was to stand near Aden, she tried her best to back out, but Cerise held her to her promise.

"Here goes a ringer!" cried Lawrence and sent a horseshoe spinning so wildly that everyone ducked.

None of Lawrence's shoes made it even close to the stake. Cerise laughed jubilantly as she poised for throwing a shoe. Her attempts were even wilder than Lawrence's. Rebekah held her breath as Aden stepped back from the stake and aimed before throwing the iron horseshoe. She clapped wildly when his horseshoe slid into the stake, then let her hands hang limp as he gave her a solemn, sideways look. Why didn't he look happy at making such a good shot? Cerise was jumping up and down in sheer pleasure at this success for anyone, partner or not.

"Bet you can't do it again!" Cerise called to him.

"Probably not. But here goes." This time the shoe landed neatly within a width of the stake.

David and Betsy and others began to gather around to watch them.

"Your turn, Rebekah! Your turn!" exclaimed Cerise, jumping up and down, her bright pigtails bobbing.

Rebekah groaned. She'd tried to watch each one for tips but hadn't many clues yet as to how to do this tricky thing. Her first horseshoe went into a crazy spin when it left her hand. Aden put up his arms to protect himself and quickly gave her more space. The next one rolled a "fur piece," as David described it. Her last throw landed a shoe in decent range but was definitely not in scoring range. Well, at least it was over, for now.

Of course Aden won the game easily, though others, even Cerise, finally made a few points. As the game ended, Rebekah suddenly became aware of Rosemary appearing in a blue and white calico sewn in a particularly enchanting design with a pinched-in waist and flowing skirt. She fairly floated through groups of neighbors to Aden's side. As Rosemary faced Aden with one hand on her hip, the other fiddling with a loose curl by her ear, Rebekah saw that the dress had a huge drifting bow in the back. She was inclined to giggle but was able to hold it back. As she turned away to go watch Lawrence in a corn-husking competition, she distinctly heard Rosemary ask in her sweetest voice if Aden would please show her how to throw horseshoes since he was so very, very good at it.

Later, around the crowded board, Rebekah followed Cerise but placed only half as much food on her plate as did her small partner. She looked around for Aden and saw that he was talking, not to Rosemary, but to Jess Porter, the fiddler. They were leaning against one of the barn's finished walls while they ate and talked. Jess was so jovial today, very different from the day he'd started out in the chair to have two teeth taken and had ended up on the floor. They were probably talking about how he'd made his own fiddle, what kind of wood he'd used, how long it had taken. Aden had been very interested in that, had asked the man lots of questions after his teeth were out, making his answers all mumbled.

David Mayfield made a fine speech following supper. He stood on an upturned barrel and got quite red in the face trying to hold back emotions as he thanked his neighbors for their help. "And you children, too," he added. "A man couldn't be more blessed than to have God seeing him through hard times. My wife, Betsy. What would I have done without her?" He sought her round, merry face among the women hovering near the table in case they were needed. "And my special new friends, Aden and Rebekah Robards," he said, readily finding Aden, having to look some for Rebekah. "Ah, there you are, Rebekah. This lady's been picking apples day after day. And Aden, Isaac Aden, did you people know that's his whole given name? Well, Aden's the one saved my horses so he's—you know how I feel, Son! Leastways, I hope you do. Well—" David lifted his hands palms up in a gesture of helplessness as he picked out good loving faces of the Moffatts, Sheriff Bozeman, and all the rest. There was no way he could thank everyone adequately. "It's been a tough year for us—and for our country—but we'll keep trusting Him," he said, lifting a hand skyward, "and helping each other out." He cleared his throat and shuffled his feet before ending with, "And now, before we make pigs of ourselves over at that loaded dessert table, let's dance and sing. Jess, where are you? Come on over, Friend!"

Jess Porter knew how to make a fiddle cry and laugh and sing. He was a small, wiry man with bright blue eyes twinkling above wrinkled, weathered cheeks. His chin was sharp and jutting, perfect for clamping his fiddle in place as his fingers twinkled along the strings, and his bow rhythmically pulled the music out. A hank of gray hair persisted in falling across his left eye, but he was adept at slinging it back without missing a beat. Frequently he'd stop to add rosin to his bow or to take a sip of apple cider placed nearby for him.

The new storage room and a room for Betsy's quilting frame had been floored in bright white pine boards, and though neither room was very large, they became popular places for a few to dance. The rest happily capered on the dirt floor, either down the wide middle or in the stalls, already studded, but not partitioned as yet.

Rebekah again looked around for Aden. She saw him talking to Lawrence, then David Mayfield, then being pulled onto that storage room floor by Rosemary in her blue and white dress, which now, in lantern light, looked more white. Why hadn't he remembered he was to dance with Rebekah? How could he forget when it had seemed so important at the time? If he had forgotten that promise, then he must also have forgotten the other words he'd said that had warmed her so at the time: *I really do love you.* In disappointment and feeling somewhat lost, she hugged herself, realizing for the first time she never had put on her sweater. Quietly she edged farther into the shadows.

Betsy found her and slid an arm around her waist. "If you're feeling jealous of my Rosemary, I apologize for her," she said quietly. "She's a born flirt. I don't know what I'm going to do with her. But you know, Rebekah, that's all it is. Just as I'm beginning to see you two warm to each other, please don't let my girl throw you off."

Rebekah shrugged and smiled down at her friend. "Of course not," she said with as much nonchalance as possible, though for some reason a hard lump had formed in her throat. Somehow she knew there was more to Aden's behavior than responding to Rosemary's flirtatiousness. Aden didn't flirt. In all the places they'd been and with clients who did sometimes try to win a wink when they asked for appointments, he'd never given in to them that Rebekah had seen. Of course at one time she'd almost wished he would. Then it would have made it easier for her to leave. Now she didn't want to leave. She realized sharply on this cool October night how very much she wanted to stay—and not as a washerwoman and cook, but as Isaac Aden's wife.

"Come on, Rebekah! You have to dance with me!" cried Cerise, grabbing her hand.

"Oh, no, Cerise, no!" She pulled back, though the child was strong. Rebekah looked to Betsy for help, but Betsy only smiled and turned her palms up.

Cerise, it turned out, was not so much interested in dancing with Rebekah herself as in pairing her with Isaac Aden Robards. Once she'd placed Rebekah's hand in Aden's, she giggled and scooted away. Rebekah tried to withdraw her hand, not wanting to be in a position of begging for a dance. Isaac Aden tightened his grip. She looked up and was overwhelmed with the sadness in his eyes. What could be wrong? He smiled tensely and began to lead her to the tune of "Beautiful Dreamer," which Jess was whining out in style. Rebekah could see that the smile didn't reach his eyes.

Something stopped her from asking what was wrong. Maybe she didn't want to know. She clung to his hand and pretended all was well, said something about Jess's fiddling, listened to Aden talk about things that seemed utterly unimportant right now, such as whether or not President Arthur would come to Atlanta for the exposition. Who cares? What mattered was why all the time he was talking, he was studying her face in the oddest way, as if maybe she were wearing a mask. Wasn't it only a few hours ago that he had kissed her beside their wagon and his smile had been so admiring? What had happened since then?

The party was breaking up. Rebekah was eager to leave the misery of a happy party that had turned out to be so awful. At the same time, she dreaded being alone with Aden. She'd never seen him in such a mood, not even months ago when she'd sold Banner. Never had he been quite so glum in a hard sort of way. She went inside to return the empty cake plate she'd borrowed. Mayfield girls giggled with hilarity as they bombarded each other with wet dishcloths while supposedly cleaning the kitchen. Betsy Mayfield bumbled in the door behind Rebekah, who turned to help her hostess relieve herself of an armload of dishes and baskets.

"Whew, it was a good party, don't you think, Dear?" puffed Betsy, swiping the back of one hand across her brow.

Without noticing Rebekah's slowness to reply, Betsy reached in her apron pocket and pulled out an envelope. "I almost forgot you had this piece of mail. It's been such an exciting day! Thank you for all your help. Without you and Aden— well, we just wouldn't make it, I'm sure. Now you run on. I saw Aden out there looking sort of somber and displaced. He's probably tired to the very bone. You take him home and treat him tenderly, you hear?"

Rebekah smiled the best she could. "You're sure you don't want me to help in here?" she asked almost hopefully. But Betsy shook her head and gave her a little shove toward the door.

"'Night, Rebekah!" sang out all the girls. All the girls, that is, except Rosemary, who, Rebekah discovered, was still outside resweeping the storage room floor for something like the third time. Some other time maybe she could smile at Rosemary's ploys, but right now nothing was very funny.

Contrary to her fears of his silence, Aden seemed bent on making conversation as they walked to their wagon after the party. Mr. Banks had told him about the marvelous success of the Knights of Labor, who were pushing for an eight-hour working day and trying to end child labor. "We haven't either one had to experience the horrors of child labor so really have no idea how bad it is," he said. "But up north there's lots of that, in the industrial areas. I'm not sure I like this big union trying to tell everyone whether they can strike or not, sort of taking over some of the freedoms of the workers. But they are fighting for the workers' rights and especially children—and women—who can't take up for themselves."

He talked much more than usual after having avoided her all evening. Then finally, when they reached the wagon, he looked down at his feet, grunted, and turned away abruptly. "I'll see about the horses," he said.

"Aden, I don't know what's wrong—"

"We'll talk in the morning," he said heavily and disappeared into the darkness, not even helping her climb into the wagon. Certainly was no fairy-tale ending to the nice party.

With bitter disappointment, she realized he'd never even commented on her caramel cake. Had he not liked it? Had he not even eaten any? Well, at least somebody liked it. The plate had been empty.

As she prepared for bed, she remembered suddenly that she'd promised herself—and God—that she'd tell Aden about the money before she slept tonight. *Oh, no, I can't! Not now! Things are bad enough without adding that. In the morning, Lord, in the morning.*

She hardly slept all night and felt her prayers were helpless, totally ineffective. After knowing the joy of talking to God, she missed it so much. Why was God not listening any longer?

As soon as she was dressed the next morning, she went to her hiding place to pull out the now-hated sock. It wasn't there! She dug frantically, dumped a whole box of personal belongings, breaking out in a sweat as she realized it simply was not there. In her characteristic way, when things became too frantic or ominous, she spoke out loud to herself: "Oh, now, where can it be? How could I have lost it? What will I do now?"

She had not an inkling of his approach. But now Aden was at the wagon's flap opening. "Is this what you're looking for?" he asked in a voice of steel. She whirled so quickly that her dress upset odds and ends, which went clattering to the board floor. In his hand was the dreaded sock, bulging with its stolen contents.

All the speeches she'd rehearsed, all the requests for forgiveness, pleas for understanding, seemed of no good whatsoever. She gripped the folds of her skirt as she attempted to stand in the tiny space. What was there to say?

"I suppose you were about to tell me," he said, stepping back.

She clambered down, missing sharply his offered hand, which would have been there a few hours ago. "I–I meant to, yes."

"You just hadn't gotten around to it." His voice was too calm, too steady.

"That's right. I wanted to. I've prayed God would—"

"Rebekah!" He grated out her name as if it hurt to say it. "Don't blame God for any of this. I could use some of your own words from a few months back. Don't bring God into this. This was your doing, entirely your own doing."

"I know. I didn't mean—"

He was so close to her now, she could see his nostrils flare, a nerve in his tensed jaw quivering. Then he was towering over her, waving that awful sock right in her face. "I've known all along you kept some of Banner's money. I've known all along you were cheating! Only I tried not to believe it. I didn't want to believe it. But when I found this, there was no escaping the truth. Just what were you going to do with this money? I'd have given you money for your parents if you'd asked. I'd have given you money for clothes or books or whatever you wanted. Oh, Rebekah, I wanted you to trust me, and instead you've totally dishonored every pact we made with each other! Here. This is yours. I didn't even get through counting it. It doesn't matter. However much is here, you take it. And be satisfied," he finished with a break in his voice.

"No. No, I don't want it!" She shoved it back at him, but he refused to hold it. He turned away, looked around camp almost as if he were hunting for something, then suddenly leaped on Jake, whom he'd already saddled, and rode away without another word.

She watched him disappear, riding toward town. Even at a distance there was no mistaking Isaac Aden Robards's fury. She looked down at her shaking hands still holding that sock full of money that felt now like—like thirty pieces of silver, nonreturnable.

She slumped to the ground on her knees and crumpled forward. Silver dollars fell out of the sock, and she didn't care.

Through the agony of her sobs, she heard a voice clearly prodding her, *Have patience, My child. Don't give up yet. He had patience with you, remember?* But she also heard her own flesh crying, "How dare he give me no chance to explain! How dare he jump on me so hard as if I'm the first person ever to make a mistake! He wouldn't listen, he who's preached and preached to me about every sinner's having a second chance!" When finally she stood up, she left the money lying there as she prepared breakfast, not knowing whether or not he was coming back. He'd already built a fire and fetched a bucket of water, but he'd had nothing to eat.

An hour, then two hours, went by with no splattering of hooves approaching. Should she ride Jolly into town and arrive at work as usual? But, then, of course not. This was Saturday. So where had Aden gone? What was to become of them? She felt a churning sensation in her stomach. She climbed back in the wagon and dropped to her knees to pray. *Lord, I have sinned against You, and I have no excuses. Oh, Father, how I crave Your forgiveness. Sir—please—could I begin again?*

As her tears flowed, so came peace into her heart. Aden would never forgive her; she'd hurt him too badly. She saw no way to convince him she was a different person from the silly, selfish girl he'd married on Thornapple's porch. But— God would forgive her, had already. God had forgiven her!

When she at last tried to stand, her legs were so cramped that she ended up sitting down instead. Numbly, she began setting to rights the confusion she'd caused earlier when she searched for the sock of money. Then she straightened out the dress she'd worn to the party. Might as well pack it away, for there was no telling when she'd wear it again. But what was this crackling in one pocket? Oh, yes, the letter Betsy had given her as she left last night.

It was a letter from Father! Maybe he'd have something to

say that would lift her spirits! She ripped open the flap with a tiny wave of excitement, anything to distract her for a moment from the awful truth that she'd shattered her and Aden's chances for happiness. Several dollar bills fluttered down the front of her dress as she unfolded Father's letter. What in the world—?

Father had decided Mother really had to go back to Thornapple, even if it meant he grew cotton on shares for Mr. Jones. He was probably even now trying to get them settled there, having very little with which to settle. Yet, somehow, he'd sent her money in case she and Aden needed it in order to come "home." Aden could practice dentistry in the house, Father said. And there would be ample work for all!

This was what she'd wanted more than anything: to return to Thornapple—that is, to return to Thornapple without Aden. *But now it is different! Oh, God, do I have to go— without him?*

Finally, she wiped tears away with both hands, set her teeth firmly, and began preparations. What she had to do, she would do. At least she could help Father and Mother, even if she'd messed up everything else.

It took her an amazingly short time to set the camp to rights, leave the fire extinguished, and lay Aden's sock with every dollar of its contents intact just inside the wagon opening where he'd find it easily. She stuffed the barest necessities into a small cloth bag and looked once more at the tiny cubicle, which had been home for the past few months. There was the little table with its legs in the air, the funny little elegant table that had been part of that memorable, sweet evening. There, cradled inside it, on top of other things was her cloth bag full of colorful squares she'd woven. She picked it up and pulled out a square made of scraps from one of Betsy's dresses. Should she take her weaving? But, no, she couldn't carry everything. As she turned away, she glimpsed something white. Tugging material from underneath other things, she discovered the dress length of white lawn given her by a friend in Forsyth. Rosemary would be able to make something beautiful of it, she thought wistfully. She couldn't very well take it, and there seemed no point. She smoothed it and placed it carefully back in the stack. What she did make sure to put in her bag was the Bible Betsy Mayfield had given her. That she wanted always with her.

She jumped to the ground and looked around the camp, more worn than any other they'd occupied, more like home to her than any. Maybe because it was here that she became a true child of God. And it was here she realized how much she loved her husband. In a strange state of numbness, yet with sharpened senses, she walked along the stream until she found Jolly and, walking up to him easily, patted him on one shoulder, speaking gently to him. A frown creased her forehead. She laid her bag beside a hickory tree and went for a rope to tether Jolly securely but with plenty of room to get to some nibbles until Aden returned. When she tied him, he nuzzled his head into her chest, and her tears spattered on his nose; but she didn't notice. Retrieving her bag, she walked determinedly out of camp, heading toward the road and Cornelia.

twelve

"Where you going?" Cerise suddenly popped in front of her dressed in those floppy overalls, but with shoes on now for this chilly day and a sweater.

"I'm—going to town," hedged Rebekah.

"With that bag full of stuff?" Cerise ran along, trying to keep pace. She plucked at Rebekah's sleeve. "Why all the stuff?"

Rebekah stopped and looked Cerise in the eyes. Oh, how to explain!

"Where are you really going? It's Saturday, you know." Cerise's brown eyes had widened in alarm.

"I'm—leaving. For good," said Rebekah, starting on, her head bent forward to her task. "Just tell—tell everyone—explain to them—"

"Rebekah, you come and explain! You can't leave. Where are you going anyway? Where—where's Aden? I thought—"

Rebekah paused again, looking back to the appled hill fringed at its base with red sweet gum and bright yellow hickories. The hill hid the Mayfields' cozy house, their new barn. So many good times she'd enjoyed there. Maybe she should—but no! She'd lose her nerve if Betsy started in on her. She plodded on.

But Cerise wouldn't give up.

"You've got to tell everybody good-bye!" Tears exploded down her cheeks. "You can't go like this! You're—you're my friend, Rebekah!" Suddenly she dashed at Rebekah and grabbed her around the waist as best she could, Rebekah being cumbered with her knobby bag.

Rebekah groaned, put her bag down, and wound her arms

around Cerise's slender frame, leaning over to touch her cheek to the little girl's hair. "I'm glad we could be friends. And—you'll always be so special to me. But I have to go. I'll write to you," she said, struggling to be firm.

Cerise stiffened then pulled back. Standing squarely in front of Rebekah, she placed her hands on her hips, looking almost comically like her mother when she laid down the law. "You can't go right now, Rebekah! Don't you realize it's about to freeze and we're going to lose all the Shockleys still on the trees if we can't get them picked? Everyone's picking apples like crazy except Mama, and I came to see if you would come help, too. You can't leave us right now! You just can't!"

Rebekah looked at Cerise, a tumble of red-brown hair framing her tear-stained intense face, then at her own bulging bag by the roadside. "All right—help me put this under some bushes so I can get it later. I'll go help for a few hours before I go." She had no idea when her train left, but she'd have to risk missing it, maybe having to spend the night on a bench at the station. She would not spend one more night in Aden's wagon.

As they walked through the orchard, Rebekah said, "I don't hear a thing. There aren't any pickers out here, Cerise."

"Oh, yes, there are, too! The Shockleys are in the far orchard, t'other side of the house."

"We have to go by the house?" Rebekah paused, gripping folds of her skirt. Why did she not want to talk to Betsy? Wasn't it instead that she wanted very much to talk to Betsy? She needed to talk to Betsy!

"It's the best way to get there," said Cerise, looking at her friend curiously.

"Might as well stop by then and see your mama a minute," said Rebekah decisively.

The minute Betsy saw her face, she dusted flour from her hands and held out her arms as if she knew everything.

"Run on to the picking, Cerise," she said. "I need Rebekah to help me here. You will, won't you, Rebekah?"

"I—if you need me. Sure."

Cerise complained but soon ran out the door. As soon as she was gone, Betsy nudged Rebekah into a chair at the table and sat down opposite her. "For once, we need to talk without doing anything," she said. "Now tell me what is going on. I've already heard Aden's version, but I want to hear yours."

"You've heard Aden's?" She leaned forward, her heart thudding.

"Yes. I—he came this morning early. He told me—well, I want to hear it in your words 'fore I do any quoting. But—I can tell you this much—it's one of the few times I've seen a man cry. And he wasn't just crying. He was weeping. His heart is broken, Child."

"I know," she said, her voice trembling as she put her hands to her face. "I've ruined everything just as we were becoming so happy. But I know he can never forgive me so I—the letter you gave me was from Father inviting me to come home."

Betsy peeled Rebekah's hands away from her face and peered into her eyes. "Is that what you want? To go home? Because it isn't what Aden wants. He's brokenhearted, not because of what you did, but because of your motives, because he thinks you want to leave him."

"Oh, I don't want to! But I must!" Rebekah pulled her hands away to cover her face again; she felt so ashamed before her friend. "I can't stay any longer; I've done such terrible things. Oh, Betsy, I so wanted to make it right. I wanted to tell him all about it and tell him—but I didn't know how! I didn't want the money any longer. I hated it! I just wanted—him to understand."

"Then if you want to tell him, you'd best figure out a way." Betsy stood up. "Aden's out there in the orchard somewhere picking apples. You go see if you can't help. I'll be here cooking—and praying. Go on now! God's given you an opportunity. Don't flub it!"

Rebekah considered her options. If she wanted something so terrifically much, then why not try? What could it hurt? *Could Betsy possibly be right? Could Isaac Aden Robards still love me?*

Slowly she pushed her chair back and stood, answering Betsy's encouraging smile with a teary one of her own.

Rebekah started across the porch, saw the well bucket hanging ready to dip water, another empty pail ready for use on a chair nearby. It was turning cold, as Cerise had said, probably going to freeze tonight. Maybe nobody would be in the least bit thirsty. But—she'd take water anyway. The rope squeaked as she let the bucket down, and she heard a splash as it hit water. Behind her, Betsy said softly, "Here's a ladle we use, Honey."

Rebekah walked slowly when she came to rows of Shockley trees laden with small, dull russet apples. Mayfield pickers could be heard in the distance singing and calling to each other from various positions, each trying to fill his bag first. Suddenly, as she stood there shading her eyes with one hand, all the singing and joking stopped. She heard only a faint buzz, almost like summer bees working, as apples were snatched and added to others in gunnysacks. The trees' leafy foliage had turned yellow, and many leaves had fallen. She should be able to spot Aden and his long legs without any trouble. But where was he? She began walking slowly between the trees, heart thudding against her ribs. Adjusting her bucket from one hand to another, she spilled cold water down the side of her dress.

Then she saw him far down a row of trees striding toward her, his face sober, his jaw shadowed by a night's growth of whiskers. She firmed her chin against an onslaught of tears at the sight of him, but her eyes stung all the same. He had cried for her! So why shouldn't she cry for him? Carefully she set her bucket down in orchard grass.

Aden stopped a few feet away, folded his arms across his chest, scuffed one shoe in the browning grass.

She hung her head and licked her salty lips, trying to think what to say, desperately wanting to explain everything in a way he would understand. But Aden spoke first.

"I–I'm sorry, Rebekah. I didn't—there's so much I didn't know."

"You're sorry?" She looked up quickly. "No, no! It isn't your fault. It's every bit my own fault. But, Aden—I've changed!"

He smiled hugely then, his strong white teeth flashing. It was as if the sun had just burst through a tremendous bank of snow clouds. His shoulders visibly relaxed. "Betsy told me! I wish I'd known. But it doesn't matter. I know it now. I'm so happy, Rebekah! You'll never make any other decision that's anywhere near as important as deciding to follow Jesus." He held his hands out toward her, then let them drop straight by his sides.

"I've got Jesus joy now," she said, smiling through her tears. "No matter what happens, He'll go with me."

For an eternity they stood there beside the bucket of water, Aden swiping a hand through his thick hair, then hooking his thumbs in the corners of his pockets, Rebekah wrapping her arms around herself.

"I'm sorry about everything, Aden," she said finally, her voice breaking. "I'm so sorry!"

"Does that mean you're leaving?" he asked huskily.

"That depends, I guess, on—"

"On what, Rebekah?" he asked, taking a step toward her.

"Well—I know this isn't quite the way the story goes, but—anyway—" She leaned over and dipped a ladle full of water. "Isaac, would you allow me to give you water—and—and your horses also?"

When he was silent, she looked up anxiously. He was smiling, but there was a glint of tears in his eyes. Closing the gap between them, he leaned over so his lips could connect with her offered ladle, and he placed his hands firmly over hers to steady the vessel. Keeping his gaze on her face, he took a huge swallow, even letting water run down his chin and splash down the front of his shirt.

"My horses aren't here right now. But I accept for them, too," he said, his blue eyes sparkling. "We are all very thirsty, especially me."

Somehow the ladle landed several feet away, and the bucket spilled over, watering a patch of dried thistle. They didn't notice. They were wrapped in each other's arms, each absorbing the joy and warmth of the other. "I love you," he whispered against her tear-dampened cheek, and in answer she raised her lips to his.

"I love you, too," she said a few minutes later, snuggling under his chin.

"Oh, Rebekah, I thought I was losing you! I've prayed so hard you'd want to stay, but I thought I must have made a terrible mistake, that God must never have intended for me to do anything but travel alone up and down the roads in my wagon." He gripped her shoulders and held her away so he could study her face. "You know, I—uhm—I have to be a dentist"—she nodded—"and I have to tell God's good news"—she nodded again—"but—I see now that He doesn't necessarily mean me to keep traveling on and on. Here, look at this."

His fingers fumbled as he slid a folded document from his shirt pocket.

"What is that?"

"It's a deed," he answered.

"A deed?"

"To some property a few miles from here. I thought—a few weeks ago—you were liking it here, liking the May-fields, and maybe—"

"I was liking you, too," she supplied with a saucy smile.

"So I thought maybe we—"

"Could build a house," she finished for him.

"Well?" He lifted one eyebrow as only he could do.

"I had a letter yesterday from Father," she said, running the tip of a finger along the line of his briary jaw.

"Oh." He sobered instantly. "How are they?"

"Mother keeps getting worse. She—can't be satisfied, always wants to go home. So—Father has corresponded with Mr. Jones, and they've agreed for him to sharecrop a few acres and live in the house at Thornapple. You know, Mr. Jones bought Thornapple."

"And—you want to go back there to help?" he asked quietly.

A hawk flew in wide circles above the orchard. Voices of the Mayfields hummed in the distance. One of the dogs let out a playful bark.

"Do you want to go back there?" he repeated urgently.

"Not alone," she answered. And then she said, "No, I don't want to go back there, not to stay. Aden, what I really want is home—but not that home anymore. What I want is our home, yours and mine. With you being 'the repairer of the breach' and I your assistant. And near here would be absolutely wonderful. I love it here!"

An explosion of giggles crackled from a nearby tree, and Cerise jumped out from behind its trunk. "You're staying!" she cried, clapping her hands.

From several trees away, Rosemary called, "Cerise, shame on you for eavesdropping!"

But Isaac and Rebekah were oblivious to any disturbance.

"We could go down soon and see your parents, see how your mother is and if there's anything we can do to help," he said.

"Thank you. I—don't know how Father will take care of everything."

Isaac Aden framed her face with his hands. "We will do whatever we need to do," he said firmly.

"But I hope we can be back here for New Year's," she said. "Because we need to start the new year off camping on our very own place. Maybe—do you think when we finish saving the apples you could take me to see our land?"

He laughed and let out a spontaneous whoop as he picked her up and spun her around.

≈

In years to come, Isaac Aden would tell his children he married their mother because her name was Rebekah. And Rebekah would tell them she sure was glad her parents named her Rebekah. But after she returned to the kitchen or her garden, Isaac Aden would wink at the children and say, "I'd have married that woman if her name had been Izziatorus Opalanckus." Every time he said it, he chose a more difficult name, and the children rolled with laughter.

A Letter To Our Readers

Dear Reader:

In order that we might better contribute to your reading enjoyment, we would appreciate your taking a few minutes to respond to the following questions. We welcome your comments and read each form and letter we receive. When completed, please return to the following:

Rebecca Germany, Fiction Editor
Heartsong Presents
PO Box 719
Uhrichsville, Ohio 44683

1. Did you enjoy reading *Her Name Was Rebekah* by Brenda Knight Graham?
   ❏ Very much! I would like to see more books by this author!
   ❏ Moderately. I would have enjoyed it more if

   _____

   _____

2. Are you a member of **Heartsong Presents**? Yes ❏ No ❏
   If no, where did you purchase this book?_____

   _____

3. How would you rate, on a scale from 1 (poor) to 5 (superior), the cover design?_____

4. On a scale from 1 (poor) to 10 (superior), please rate the following elements.

   _____ Heroine   _____ Plot

   _____ Hero   _____ Inspirational theme

   _____ Setting   _____ Secondary characters

5. These characters were special because_____
   _____
   _____

6. How has this book inspired your life?_____
   _____
   _____

7. What settings would you like to see covered in future
   Heartsong Presents books?_____
   _____
   _____

8. What are some inspirational themes you would like to see
   treated in future books?_____
   _____
   _____

9. Would you be interested in reading other **Heartsong
   Presents** titles?   Yes ☐   No ☐

10. Please check your age range:
    ☐ Under 18   ☐ 18-24   ☐ 25-34
    ☐ 35-45   ☐ 46-55   ☐ Over 55

Name _____

Occupation _____

Address _____

City _____ State _____ Zip _____

Email _____

·····Heart♥ng·····

HEARTSONG PRESENTS TITLES AVAILABLE NOW:

(If ordering from this page, please remember to include it with the order form.)

Presents

Great Inspirational Romance at a Great Price!

Heartsong Presents books are inspirational romances in contemporary and historical settings, designed to give you an enjoyable, spirit-lifting reading experience. You can choose wonderfully written titles from some of today's best authors like Peggy Darty, Sally Laity, Tracie Peterson, Colleen L. Reece, Debra White Smith, and many others.

When ordering quantities less than twelve, above titles are $3.25 each.
Not all titles may be available at time of order.